The
Lighthouse
Keeper

Also by James Michael Pratt

The Last Valentine

THE
LIGHTHOUSE
KEEPER

JAMES MICHAEL
PRATT

ST. MARTIN'S PRESS
NEW YORK

ISBN 0-312-24113-5

Design by Maureen Troy

*Dedicated to the memory of the man who inspired this
story, Grant L. Pratt Sr., my father, and soldier of the First
Armored Division, "Old Ironsides," campaigns in
North Africa and Italy during World War II.
The example he set before me guides my steps
and lights my path to this day.*

Acknowledgments

I WOULD like to express my gratitude to the memory of men who have so fully lived with "light" that they have ever been an inspiration to me through the years. The inspiration I have gained from knowing them directly influenced the message of this book.

First, with grateful appreciation and in memory of the strength and character of a youthful friend, Michael Alan Carlisle, who surrendered his life in the service of others in San Salvador in 1973 at the age of twenty, I still owe a debt of gratitude. His living example in our youth added one more stone to the pillars of moral courage and strength which sustain me.

Holy scripture reads: "No greater love hath a man than this, than to give his life for his fellow man." Michael Carlisle was willing to follow a greater light than his own. Thank you, Mike. I told you, I wouldn't forget.

And there is that very special Mike, my son, who is living with dignity and honor in his youth, as did his namesake. He is kind, loving to those around him, and generous to his friends. It takes a special kind of boy to be willing to follow "the light of the world" in this day and age of temptation and trials. I honor and respect him for that light he lives in and shares with others.

To my friend and executive editor Jennifer Enderlin at St. Martin's Press, I offer a special thanks. She is ever a talented and enthusiastic supporter of fiction with a message, and she is genuine and honest in her profession.

My thanks once again to literary managers Kenneth J. Atchity and Chi Li Wong of Atchity Entertainment International, Inc., of Los Angeles and New York, who dedicate themselves to bettering our profession and, by so doing, bring value and entertainment to the reader and moviegoers. They possess the "big picture" while encouraging the dreams of those they represent. Also, a special thanks to my friend Andrea McKeown, AEI Executive Editor, who offered valuable advice and assistance in the initial proposal for *The Lighthouse Keeper.*

To Leo Weidner, personal coach and "success guru," I want to offer my everlasting appreciation for taking what you found in 1997 and making him a better man through expert and wise counsel. I love ya, man!

To my long-suffering wife, Jeanne, I love you. Thanks for enduring all the lean times to help me fulfill this dream of mine—being part of the solution and a light to a world often living in the shadows at midday.

My love and adoration also goes to my "read-a-holic" daughter, Amy, who helps keep me inspired to write uplifting themes. She reminds me why I write and for whom.

Finally, I want to thank the many readers who write to me

offering kind words for *The Last Valentine* and who have shared with me their anxious anticipation for my next book. To them I offer *The Lighthouse Keeper* with gratitude for the inspiration and encouragement they have given me.

THE

LIGHTHOUSE

KEEPER

Prologue

KATHLEEN HAD been painting for hours but finally had to put the paint brush down. Each stroke of the brush had been a futile attempt to forget his pain, and hers.

Walking from the easel to the open door of the cottage attached to the Port Hope Lighthouse, she leaned against its door post and watched as the lonely lighthouse keeper sat in his wheelchair gazing out to sea. She knew what he was thinking. It was this place that had first brought him to his beloved Anna more than fifty years before.

She struggled with the belief that her father was going to die, not the strong, self-reliant, well-loved lighthouse keeper. She had never known a mother but for the faintest of memories. And the memory was a gleaming smile of a lovely face bending over to kiss her soft toddler cheeks on one of hundreds of nights she had been tucked into bed by her.

He was all she had. Of course there was her own dear family, her husband Tony, and sweet children back on Nantucket, but no man matched this man, her father.

She went back to the canvas, stumped. *Almost there,* she thought. To finish the cove scene and the pier was all that was required to make this painting a tribute and gift to her father. She desperately wanted him to see it completed before . . . Those words she couldn't say, couldn't think about, made it as hard to finish the painting as it did to contemplate them.

If she finished the painting, maybe he, too, would come to an end.

1

THE OCEAN never changed. Maybe that's why Peter O'Banyon loved it so very much. The ebb and flow of her vast tides were reliable. He aged, but she stayed the same. Her waves, currents, and perpetual deepness awed him; they were never ending, like eternity. Eternity meant more to him now that he was about to set foot upon its shore.

A gentle warm breeze tussled his silvery hair, and his eyes closed meditatively. It was as if Uncle Billie had just patted him on the head, "You're becomin' a right smart and handsome lad, Peter. It makes me proud. Go on now, enjoy your day with Anna."

On the inside, it felt like 1942, and the cliff upon which he now sat was then a rolling hill of grasses and sand that tumbled down to the beach. It had not been eroded by time—not a shear drop as it now was.

Peter opened his eyes and gazed down to his blanket-covered lap. His daughter had laid the old lighthouse logbook and a pen there as he had asked. He reached into his overcoat pocket and pulled a crumpled and considerably age-worn letter from a time-yellowed envelope.

With his free hand, though trembling, he shuffled through the tattered and frayed logbook until he found the final blank page at the end. Placing the letter and envelope in the crease for a page marker, he began to methodically spell out his final impressions to bring this lighthouse logbook to a seamless conclusion:

"Port Hope Island Lighthouse is empty now except for the occasional tourist, who on Saturday mornings pays the state-park fee of $3.50 to climb the stairs and look out over the ocean from the majestic cliff home that I have known. I first called it home with my Uncle Billie, then with my beloved Anna. But its very emptiness offers a poetic soliloquy of sorts, if one listens hard enough.

"It is as if the old lighthouse keeper is haunting the halls, striking a match to the 1500-watt-candlepower oil lantern that used to cast a beam across the bay to guide so many seafarers safely to shore. None of the mariners from the past would have ever seen the lightkeeper, but I grew up knowing they saw his flame. One hundred times one thousand must have been grateful to see it there burning brightly during the gales and storms that lashed the New England coast from the 1920s to 1943 when he faithfully manned his watch.

"The lighthouse stood silently majestic then as it does now, a pinprick of illumination in the deep blue darkness, but its message was loud enough then. 'Aye, laddie,' he would say to me, 'A lightkeeper never knows who he touches with the toil of his hands while keepin' the flame alive.'

"The old light went out with him some fifty-five years ago. A newer, more powerful beacon has been built inland with radar navigation, making the old Port Hope Lighthouse obsolete. I often wondered if my uncle, the seasoned seafarer, ever felt like he too was becoming 'obsolete,' a relic of bygone times—when individual men made such a difference; when machines where no match for their brains or brawn.

"William Robert O'Banyon, 'Uncle Billie,' made me what I was, what I became. From a small boy of ten, I grew up with him on the tiny outer island off Massachusetts' larger, more famous Nantucket. He was my 'schoolmaster of life,' as he often reminded me.

"All I know now, as I look back, is if Uncle Billie was my original 'schoolmaster,' then Anna was the one who brought to me the gentleness and love for life I have known. I never knew, nor ever wanted to know, another like her.

"I realize now, as I gaze down to the bay, jotting these notes in the lighthouse log, that perhaps it is my final farewell to this place that I have loved so well."

Peter O'Banyon set the habitually handled, black, leather-bound logbook on his lap. His daughter had made sure he was comfortable, a blanket covering his shoulders as he sat in the wheelchair eyeing the splendor of twilight. This was his favorite time of day, though at times it seemed a melancholy hour, watching the fading sun turn a luminescent blue sea into a shimmering yellow, then back to deep blueness. From the southern point of the island, where the lighthouse sat, he had a perfect advantage to enjoy sunrise or sunset. Now, sunset accented the deep blueness that also seemed to fill his soul.

He looked up into the sky and watched the progeny from seagulls which had flown overhead five decades before and was soothed by the noisy cacophony as they were carried on their wings by a light offshore breeze.

Some things never change, he thought. It amused him now

to watch the seabirds swoop down from the cliffside heights to the beach and pier below, squawking and grousing over bits and pieces of churned up sea life that washed to shore. "I knew your great-great grandparents," he said aloud, as if they could understand that *his* knowing their past could make the present all the more interesting to them. *People are like seagulls,* he thought.

Memory was to Peter as a resuscitating breath was to the dying. He relied heavily upon it. It awakened all that was good, the golden strands of life, all that had been right in living fully without regret. And, oh, how good, but brief, it had been with Anna.

He focused intently on the pier now as he had for fifty-seven full years of Saturdays at sunset. He never missed his rendezvous, even though the last few years of sickness from cancer had him confined to bed rest at his daughter Kathleen's home on Nantucket Island. Now the doctors had given him weeks, at best, but with their permission and Kathleen's loving understanding, she had brought him here once more.

Peter pulled the withered letter from the logbook pages marking his final entry. He looked down on it. His watering eyes couldn't read the words, but he had them memorized now, and he clutched the yellowed paper as if it were holy script—it had indeed seemed so to him.

"What happened?" he whispered to himself as he held his hands out and witnessed the wear of time. "I was nineteen just yesterday." It seemed like yesterday, anyway. No matter. Inside was where Anna lived, and he was forever young there.

He was happy to be here though. As sick as he had been for two years and as tired and heavy with age as he sometimes felt, a sudden surge of youth and feeling of liveliness coursed through him now.

His daughter, Kathleen, waved to him from the top of the lighthouse. "I'm turning on the lights, Dad," she called out.

He nodded and smiled. It was the ritual. The lights would shine on the pier and then he would focus his wrinkled eyes and maybe see Anna there, dancing once again.

If he looked hard enough, he could see himself running along the beach . . . with her.

Laughing.

Holding hands.

Full of the joy young love brings. No care for tomorrow.

Just now.

They would tumble into the surf, kiss, and run some more, dodging the foamy breakers as they rolled in, and then playfully jump into them.

He had been nineteen, she eighteen. . . .

It was wartime, but also time for love.

He turned to look for his daughter, who had brought him home to the lighthouse, and sighed. He wanted just a little more time, just in case Anna had come.

Perhaps he should turn back to face the pier once more. If his watering eyes could focus well enough, he might imagine her standing there, the way she would each Saturday morning on the antiquated dock.

He drank deeply of the cool sea air. In his mind's eye she was waving, smiling, the long tresses of crimson cascading down to her shoulders. She seemed to beckon him to join her for a swim once more. She waved. He stood on the hill looking down.

Should he wave back? Dare he indulge his imagination? He

could smile though. She always smiled back—at least in his mind.

No. He would venture a wave this time. It was getting late in the number of years they greeted each other thus, Saturday after Saturday, his special day of the week to be alone with her.

He took his cap off and held it high over his head and waved. But she was gone like so many mirages.

He looked down and upon his lap was the lighthouse journal—the logbook. He moved his hand over the pages, turning them slowly and gently.

"Then life is not a dream. Love has endured this probation without them. Uncle Billie and Anna were and are real," he whispered to himself.

"Dad! I'll be right down to get you," Kathleen, his daughter, called from the lighthouse window.

"No hurry," he offered with a cough and wave of the hand. "I'm fine. Real good," he weakly called back. *Real good,* he thought as his mind played tricks on him again.

"Anna? Is that you?" he softly asked as he focused once more on the pier below.

2

P ETER'S VISION of that boyhood day broke with the
sounds of his daughter's footsteps. "Did I ever tell you
how I first met your mother?" he asked Kathleen.

"Dad, I can't even sneak up on you, can I?" she replied,
hugging his slender frame from behind. "Yes, you've told me.
It's a beautiful story. We'd better go in. You'll catch your death
of cold."

"Hah! So I'm going to die from a cold, huh?" He laughed.

"Dad, that's not fair. I'm supposed to be sad. Knock it off,"
she moaned.

"I love you, darling," he said as he looked out over the bay.
"You really handle that big light up there well," he said.

"I had a good teacher," Kathleen replied, taking the wheelchair by the handles. "Did you see her tonight?"

"Aye, lass, that I did," Peter answered in the Irish brogue
of his Uncle Billie. "If ya take me in, and brew me a warm
milk, and make me that fine bread puddin' of yours, I'll tell
ya something else I saw."

"Dad!" Kathleen giggled with moisture coming suddenly to her eyes. Her father was as charming, as whole, and as real on the inside as he ever had been. It surprised her to see this much life in him. She expected solemnity and sadness to accompany the inevitable, but somehow he hung on, cheering her up. "Your little darlin' will fix ya right up," she answered with throaty emotion as she wheeled him into the lighthouse parlor.

Peter looked down at the yellowed letter he still clutched in his hand. It had been written long ago, and now it was time to make sure Kathleen, his only child, knew the story behind it well. It was his biggest concern now that time was short. He folded it shakily, but neatly, putting it back into the tattered, time-tinctured envelope, and then replaced it inside his coat pocket. Kathleen helped him up and then into the easy chair by the bay window. He could sit and look out to the ocean and follow the beam from the lighthouse easily. The puffy, billowing sheets had all disappeared.

"It's a beautiful night. I want to die on such a beautiful night," he voiced softly.

"Please don't talk like that," implored Kathleen as she eased him into the chair.

"I'm tired and miss your mom," he answered simply.

"I know you do, Dad."

"Funny thing is, every time I come here I feel as alive inside as if it were yesterday when I first arrived with Uncle Billie. When you asked if I saw her tonight, did I tell you I saw something else, too?"

"Yes, Dad."

"Well, then . . . be about that warm milk and bread pudding and sit with me. I want to tell you all about it." He held the lighthouse log in his lap. He felt like the entry he had made would be his final notes to a family legacy. His uncle had been the first lighthouse keeper on Port Hope Island, and he, Peter O'Banyon, had been the last. He hoped Kathleen would understand what he would tell her this night and then he could go knowing he'd done as well as Uncle Billie would have expected.

"Here you go, Dad," Kathleen offered, handing him a small saucer of warmed milk. "The pudding is just about done."

She lifted the cup to her father's lips as he shakily cradled it with both hands. "It's good."

"Warm milk is easy to make," Kathleen smiled, taking the cup from him and setting it aside.

"It's good to be here, to be with you."

"Well, Dad, it's better than good. I'm thrilled to see you so happy. I'm glad we're here together, alone."

"The kids are okay?"

"I sent them with Tony to his folks for the weekend."

"Tony . . . is he still treating you good?"

"Well, twenty years and counting. Yeah, he's number one."

"I always liked Tony. Make sure you tell him that for me, will you?"

"You tell him yourself. We'll be back home Sunday evening."

Peter offered a weak smile to his daughter. "You tell him, okay?"

"Okay, Dad. Whatever you say. Here, let me put this blanket around you. I'm going to start a fire in the potbelly stove."

"Oh, that will be nice. Real nice. A fire was the last thing I recall from my boyhood with my parents and the first thing I remember coming to my new home here at the lighthouse with Uncle Billie in 1932."

"A fire?"

"I never really told you much about my boyhood past, did I?"

"No. You kept saying you would someday."

"It's what I saw out there tonight, sweetheart. I want to tell you about it while I have the strength."

"Please don't push yourself, Dad. You need to relax and take it easy."

"The doctor says I'll be relaxing for a very long time in a matter of days. . . ." he chortled morosely.

Kathleen frowned. "I don't suppose I can stop you, can I?" She paused at his forehead with a tender kiss. "I will sit right here beside you and listen."

She knew his storytelling wouldn't last long. His illness kept him doped up on pain medication. He'd had a long day, and sleep wouldn't wait on him. But a strange awareness and eagerness radiated from her father, and she wanted to indulge him. And then, her father began to talk.

3

I DON'T remember many details from my childhood before coming to Port Hope Island to live with Uncle Billie, but I have a few pleasant mental snapshots of days growing up in the country outside Morristown, New Jersey, with my father and mother.

There was a small bungalow next to a dairy farm, and my father worked both the dairy and delivery back in those days. A farmer from Ireland, the work suited my father well, and my mother, with all her industry, was a seamstress by trade.

Every Sunday morning, after Mass, we would pack up the 1928 Dodge delivery truck my father used for his milk route and head into the countryside for a picnic. I was ten years old in 1932 when, in the early part of April, we headed out for one of our favorite spots. I don't recall the name of the place, but there was a spring and a small creek running from it, and families would go there to relax and play. It seemed like heaven and earth had come together for one day each week—that is how I remember that time with them.

Father would take me to the creek, and we would dangle a fishing line. I don't remember seeing any fish but just being alone with him was good enough for me. I recall thinking I was the only one in the world when we were alone together.

I called my father "Da" on account of my Irish upbringing. On this particular Sunday, my Da said something that stuck with me and pretty much sums up all of my life up to that point with him and my mother.

"Peter," he said. "You're growin' into a fine young man an' I'm mighty proud. Will ye always remember one thing lad?"

I nodded.

"Then remember to thank the good Lord each day for what ye got and work like the devil to keep it. Then live yer life fit ta give it back when he asks. If ye do, he'll grant ya more and more until ya find ye are a right content man."

"I don't understand, Da," I answered. "Are you a content man?"

"Aye, son. That I am," he laughed as he tussled my hair. "It's a feelin' one has right here," he continued with a tender jab of his finger to my chest. "Do yer best son. Be everything what yer Mother and Da and the good Lord asks ye ta be. By and by you'll understand."

I was struck by his words in a way I had never been struck before. I don't know exactly why. Maybe I was old enough to remember, just mature enough to want to understand. But one thing stood out that afternoon. My Da took me by the hand and we walked, I don't know how many miles, down the country lane, and he told me all that he could about the O'Banyon family and how hard it was in County Cork until Uncle Billie came from America and took him back with him on a steamship.

Then, on our way back, he repeated those same words about finding peace and, especially, contentment. I must have been blessed that day, both to be unaware that anything could ever make me less than content and also to be blind to the awful tragedy that would so quickly come upon our little family. I wanted to make my Da so proud of me, and I remember wanting to be just like him when I grew up.

On the way to our home, I chose to ride in the back of the delivery truck. Riding in the front seat was my Da, Phillip, my mother, Shannon, and my two-year-old sister, Catherine. I liked riding in the back of the wood-panel delivery truck, hair flopping in the breeze and watching other cars going by. It was getting late in the day, and I recall it suddenly became overcast, and my father stopped the truck and threw a blanket to me. "Just a few more miles, lad. Cover up. We'll be home in no time," he said.

The weather suddenly turned nasty, and we had to stop at a railroad crossing. The wind had blown a mighty cloud of dust up, and rain began falling all at the same time. No one felt it coming; I didn't, that was for sure.

My Da started to cross the tracks when, all of a sudden, the locomotive was upon us. "Da!" I cried. Before I knew it, the truck was spun around, and I was thrown free.

It seemed everything moved in slow motion. I found myself running back to the truck, its tailgate all smashed in. I looked for my Da. The driver's door was half open. He was slumped forward and hanging out of the truck. My mother was leaning back against the seat, bleeding from a gash to her head. She was moaning and calling for me. I ran around to her and then, to my horror, a fire started underneath where the gas tank was, as I supposed.

She held up my baby sister, and I cried while trying to get her door open. My mother was desperately trying to get out, begging me to open the door and get little Catherine.

The door was stuck. I remember thinking I'll go over to the driver's side and climb in where my Da lay dead. He would want me to, I thought. As I got around to the other side, a big man, I can't remember what he looked like or who he was, pulled me back. I fought. Oh, how I fought to get free, but he held me tight! There was an explosion, and then all I remember was flames. I hit the man over and over again and then, when I was worn out, he picked me up and carried me to an ambulance. I woke up to see Uncle Billie's face staring down at me. His was the saddest face I'd ever seen to that day in my life.

"Now, I don't recall much on my childhood before those incidents. Do you understand, Kathleen?" Peter gazed out the window to the beam that shone from the lighthouse, its shaft of light illuminating the open sea. "It was the fire. Then the mighty guilt came, and then I couldn't recall a thing after that. If that had been the only fire in my life, then maybe I could have learned to be the content man my Da told me I should be. But fires there were. More of them. Many more."

A reverence for his words and a long pause caused a still hush to blend with the only sound that could be heard—a faint lapping of the waves upon the rocky beach below.

"Dad, why haven't you talked about this before?" Kathleen queried, breaking the ponderous quiet.

"I always meant to. Some things buried are hard to dig back up, I guess."

"Dad, you need some rest. Why don't you finish in the

morning. I'll make a bed for you here on the sofa, and you can watch the light until the oil burns out."

"I can't rest now," Peter coughed. "I'm in a hurry." With moist eyes, he gazed into his fair-skinned daughter's face looking for understanding. "You have her eyes," he said, reaching to touch her cheeks.

Kathleen embraced him but couldn't answer. A seizure of emotion locked the words inside that held all the deep love and devotion she felt for her father. She pulled her chair up to him and rested her head against his as he reclined back into the easy chair and stared out the window to the sea.

"Then, I came here to be with my Uncle Billie," he said.

Uncle Billie was a stern-seeming man. Circumstance must have made him that way. His life was not an easy one, but he never complained. I had grown accustomed to the quiet in the lighthouse. Not that I wasn't happy to be with my Uncle. It was just that William Robert O'Banyon was a man of few words and, for all his seeming demeanor of firmness, his words were never angry or short on wisdom. He had a way about him, though, that made me feel like I still had a connection to my Da.

Christmas day 1932 was a somber day. Uncle Billie had been alone for almost ten years, and it had been eight months since the terrible accident that had taken my family from me. But we had each other, and for Uncle Billie it seemed happier than any Christmas he had known for many, many years.

"You'll be needin' this, lad, if ye are to become a great man of the sea," he smiled to me.

"A fishing pole? It's mine? My very own?"

"Aye. Of course. Ye wouldn't think I'd buy myself another, would ye?"

"Oh, thank you, Uncle Billie," I smiled. "Can we try it out now?" I asked excitedly.

"Hold on there, laddie. What's that I see underneath the tree? The small box there," he pointed. It was an unwrapped, slender, wooden box about the size that could fit in the palm of my hand. "Go on now. Open it. Don't be shy," he said.

I fumbled with the small pine box two inches wide and six inches long, looking for a way to open it. I read a stamped "Made in Switzerland" on the back. "How does it open, Uncle Billie?" I asked in frustration.

"Here we go, lad," he said taking it from my hand and then smartly sliding the top back to reveal a shiny new pocket knife. Handing it to me, he said, "You'll need to scale and clean those fish ye catch and cut line loose from time to time."

"Thank you, Uncle Billie!" I smiled and, nearing to him, gave him the first real affectionate hug I remember.

I felt safe and thought about my Da as Uncle Billie held me tight and sighed, "Ah, you're mighty welcome, son, mighty welcome, indeed." Then he took my hand and said, "Shall we see if the fish are bitin'?"

"Are you awake, Kathleen?"

"I'm awake, Dad. It's a lovely story. I'm so glad you feel so well tonight and can be your old self," she said, still resting her head on his shoulder.

"Then I should tell you how the O'Banyons became lighthouse keepers, shouldn't I?"

"Aye, Da," she smiled and raised up to face him. "I must be the luckiest girl in the world to have had you for my father," she offered, stroking his stubble and giving him a tender kiss. "I'll be right here listening." Kathleen snuggled back against his shoulder and neck.

"And I must be the luckiest man in the world to have had two fine women in my life. My sweet Kathleen, listen well. It's your legacy I'm leaving you. The secret to contentment and ageless love is all I can give. It's all I know."

4

BILLIE O'BANYON was a twenty-nine-year-old newcomer to New York City in the summer months of 1913. He had scraped together every shilling he could to emigrate to America. After working as a merchant hand on board a British steamer for eight years, the young Irishman felt he had enough to finally make the break and find himself a small room somewhere near the docks where he had been offered a job as a warehouseman by one of his former shipmates who now was a foreman.

The city was far different from the green isle of Ireland and County Cork where he had grown up as a boy herding sheep. He recalled watching from the hills overlooking the ocean as the steamers from Liverpool would round the bend on their way out to sea for that far away land of dreams called America. *All dreams come true in America,* he thought then.

He would tend the sheep high in the rugged green hills and look up at the starry sky and wonder what it would be like to see tall buildings full of lights, and autos, lots of them, and become a very rich man making fabulous money in a factory or some other business.

He had been to a rich man's house once, when his father took his share of the wool sale to Mr. Dabney. He had never seen such magnificence, and he watched how his father had been treated. It had hurt him to see his Da grovel then, and he swore he would be very rich one day. He would make much more than Mr. Dabney and then he would come back to Ireland and buy Mr. Dabney out and put his Da, little brother, Phillip, and baby sister, Molly, in that house. There they would live like kings and yet treat everyone in County Cork decent and right.

The dreams of youth. So noble. So good. And heavy dreams they were—made frail only by their own weight.

In New York now, Billie had a good start. He was eager to do well, please his boss, and take his dollars and make them grow. Working twelve hours a day, six days a week, his muscular frame exuded manhood, but there was little time for socializing.

He paid his respects to God at St. Peter's Cathedral each Sunday and then would take a walk to Central Park and watch the people. He was never lonely during the week. He worked too hard and slept just as hard.

But Sundays made him wish for Ireland, the simple love and warmth of the family, a pot of stew, fresh hearth-baked bread, and a nice round mug of ale from the keg. He also recalled his wee sister's laughter (she must be all grown up now) and the admiring eyes of his younger brother, so wanting to be a man like Billie was; Da and his pipe—that pipe smell had been mighty comforting, like being tucked in as a child at night, it carried a scent of unending sameness . . . and safety; cousins and friends stopping by to say hello; Father Shannon saying, "How do ya do, laddie," as he passed by on his way to the village mass. He had been so anxious then to leave and see the world. Now?

He wrote home each Sunday. Seated in the park he would try to describe New York, its smells, its people from all over the world, the huge buildings, the sounds of sleeplessness in a city suffering from chronic insomnia.

But the loneliness dogged him on Sundays like this, a fine fall afternoon with women walking their children in strollers, cooing to their wee ones when they cried out, men and women walking arm in arm, laughing. The happiness he saw stabbed at him and mocked his every reason for coming to America.

He always knew happiness would be to make a lot of money and return to County Cork, find himself a fine lady full of fire, have children of his own, and take care of his Da, brother, and baby sister.

Sitting on the park bench and thinking about it was too much for him. He got up slowly, head bent deep in thought, and began to walk. A good strong ale at the pub down on the wharf would get him ready for the morrow and drown out his tormenting aloneness.

"Good day to you," he heard a gentle voice offer as she passed by him, parasol shielding her face from him and the setting sun.

"Oh, excuse me," Billie hurried back to her, taking off his hat. "You're very kind to greet me. Well . . . good day to you, too, Miss?"

"Kathleen. Kathleen O'Rourke. But you may call me Katie."

"You're Irish," Billie smiled broadly.

"Aye, an' you, too," she giggled. "Of course I knew that when ya sat on the bench whistling 'The Rose of Tralee.' "

"I was whistlin'?"

"Aye, an' ya whistle quite well, if ya don't mind hearing that."

Billie's heart took in the deepest azure eyes and flaming red hair he had seen since leaving the Emerald Isle over five years earlier. "I've not seen fairer beauty in all America," he blurted out in awkward elegance.

"Sir, you couldn't mean me, but if ya did, I am flattered. You haven't spoken your name," she replied blushing, smilingly.

"Aye! I am William Robert O'Banyon, County Cork, now in New York City to serve you. My friends call me Billie."

A moment of innocent silence followed as Billie looked alternately into her eyes and then down at the ground, not sure where to go from there.

"Well, I better be goin'," Katie finally offered. "The clock starts for me again at 6:00 P.M."

"You're not a regular by-the-clock workin' woman. . . . I mean you're much too fine, elegant," Billie stammered.

"I'm a simple domestic for a wealthy American family," Katie giggled. "You are so sweet, Billie O'Banyon," she said, touching him on the cheek. "I live just down o' bit on the east side. I find it o' bit lonely havin' been here two years now and barely knowin' a soul."

"May I walk ye home, then?" Billie eagerly asked.

"Aye. I'd be pleased to have a gentleman walk with me," she smiled.

5

"ONE, TWO, three. One, two, three . . ." Katie O'Rourke repeated as Billie clumsily followed her movement to the waltz she hummed.

"I'm sorry," Billie laughed. "I can do the jig," he offered. He broke free from Katie's hands and pulled out his harmonica from his vest pocket and began to dance to the tunes his lips made on the small silver instrument.

Katie clapped and grinned until they finally fell into each other's arms laughing, kissing, and searching for something that would keep them from ever saying "goodnight" or "until next Sunday," again.

Billie sat up and looked out to the sea, watching the children and families frolicking in the surf. "The children are full of life, wouldn't ye say, Katie?"

"Aye. I miss the laughter of the wee ones from home. It reminds me of them," she sighed as she started to gather up the picnic plates, saucers, and cups to put into the basket. The sand on Coney Island was still warm from the heat of the summer sun.

Billie turned to Katie suddenly and reached for her. He held her gently by her arms. She stopped what she was doing and looked intently into his penetrating gaze.

"Wouldn't it be grand ta have children?"

"What would ya mean by that, William?"

"Will ye be my bride? Will ye marry me, Kathleen O'Rourke?"

"Aye. I'll marry ye, William O'Banyon," she whispered. Her lips pressed gently against his, and the world stood still for them.

The wedding was a fine affair with kinsfolk and friends from Katie's part of the country and from Billie's County Cork. The wedding was performed by Father Flaherty from the St. Thomas Parish.

"In the name of the Father and the Son and the Holy Spirit, I pronounce you husband and wife. William, you may kiss the bride," he smiled.

Cheers and congratulations were followed with tossing rice and a stolen kiss by one of Billie's friends as the newlyweds rushed out of the small chapel in lower Manhattan and caught a cab for the train station.

A week later, at the vacation cottage of Billie's employer on Nantucket Island, far from Billie's job at the wharf, their love was finally sealed in an intimacy they had so deeply and hungrily waited to share before their marriage.

"It's grand of ye to have made me wait for this," Billie realized as he lay there, fully content to be a man.

"It was only proper and right. But aye, I've longed ta be with ya like this before. I love bein' married to you, William."

"An' ta you, Kathleen O'Banyon. Why don't we stroll along the shore one more time?" he prodded. She followed him to dress, and they slipped into the moonlight hand in hand.

"Katie, the moon, the stars, the sound of the sea, all make me want to come home ta a place like this someday. Would ye think it not grand to live a life so pleasing, so healthy from the busy life of the city? I mean for children and such?"

"Aye. It would be fine. It would be more grand than I can imagine. But what kind of work, what kind of opportunity outside the city would there be for us here?"

"I've been meaning ta tell ya. I've got this plan. It means goin' to sea. . . ."

"William, I won't be left alone!"

"Wait till ya hear me out, darlin'. Many of the lads have been joining up with the Merchant Marine. They've got big bonuses to pay and, with the war on an' all, they're supplyin' much of the munitions to the Brits and French and . . ."

"And one of them, what do they call 'em ships that go under the water and blow up the merchant ships . . . sub? . . . sub? . . ."

"Submarines."

"Aye! Submarines. Just what kind of money would ya think it's worth to me ta have ya dead or dyin' now?" she asked, eyes glistening with tears.

"Oh, Katie, Katie darlin'," he said holding her in his arms. "I did not mean ta have ya afraid or worried. I wouldn't die on ya. I'm much too stubborn for that. And with all the bonus pay, ya wouldn't have ta work. You could be about raisin' the wee ones as they come along. I won't have ya workin' like a common lass."

"I won't be able to stand it, William. What's wrong with your job at the wharf? What with all them boys runnin' off to be sailors and goin' to war, you'll be left supervisin' the whole affair. And workin'? I'll take in stitchin' before I let ya go off to get shot at. It's not our war, William," she pleaded.

"I love ya, Katie O'Banyon," he offered, gently stroking her soft skin, running his fingers lightly through the flaming red locks that cascaded down upon her shoulders.

"I love ya too much, William. That's why. That's why I won't let ya leave me for the money, for anything."

Though Billie worked from sun up to sun down at the docks, the months seemed to pass in the lingering bliss of an unending honeymoon. Their lives together in a one-room apartment near the wharf was to them as if man had carved a bit of heaven from the clouds to dance upon. He learned to waltz. She learned the jig.

Billie worked the warehouse, managing the stevedores unloading and loading ships bound for foreign ports. He was anxious to get a piece of land for his bride and for the little ones they wanted so desperately. As yet, God had not answered their prayers for children, but they were young, and time was on their side.

William had not forgotten his personal quest, either. He had an ill Da he hadn't seen in many years and a grown brother and young-woman sister to bring over from his homeland. And he had a score to settle with the landowner and financial tyrant, Mr. Dabney.

Katie took it all in, watching him work himself until he would easily fall asleep in her arms at night from the twelve-, sometimes fourteen-hour workdays. But she was proud of his determination. He was a frugal sort of man, and she admired that. The way he worked and saved gave her a sense of security she had always dreamed of.

And their little home was everything she had expected.

There would be plenty of time for the finer things, the grand vision William possessed of a small cottage by the sea here in America and then retiring to paid-for land and holdings back home in Ireland. With a man like William O'Banyon she was certain of it.

6

IT WAS 1917, and World War I had been raging on the fields of Europe and the open seas of the Atlantic for three years. President Woodrow Wilson and Congress had just declared war on Germany.

William O'Banyon held Katie tightly in his arms. They had lost one son during childbirth and a premature infant daughter from pneumonia one month after she had been born. Now Katie was pregnant again.

"I've got to be doing my duty, lass. The war won't be long now. I've held out against the pay for these years while my friends in the Merchant Marine have lined their pockets with enough to buy them a grand place of their own—freedom! Land! Think of it now, darlin'."

"What good would gold or land be without you?" she cried.

He smothered her with a final embrace. "Keep a light on for me," he managed to utter as he brought his lips to hers.

"Aye. That you can count on, William," she whispered back to him.

He boarded the ship, a merchant vessel bound for England. "God willin', I'll be back in port in a month," he shouted as he reached the top railing.

"I'll be here waitin', William," she waved back, mopping at the moisture welling in her eyes.

"Pray for us, Katie. We've got ta do this for the country. Remember me each night at midnight. I'll be in your arms, with ya in my heart ... as sure as I'm William Robert O'Banyon, I will," he shouted to her, then turned and disappeared.

Katie kept their apartment tidy in the Cork Ward, as the people called the neighborhood in southeast Manhattan. The Irish immigrants had long since organized themselves in New York by county. Katie was a County Dublin girl, but her man was from Cork, so in Cork Ward they lived.

"Good mornin' to ya, Mrs. O'Banyon. Have ya heard from Billie?" the grocer, Mr. Martin, called out as she passed by on her way to work.

"Aye, just the other day. Says he's gettin' to put in anchor at Dublin next week. He'll be payin' a visit to the folks and from there takin' a train down to make arrangements for his Da and kin ta come over to the States."

"Oh, indeed? Well, that'll be grand for ya, Katie," he returned. "Have a pleasant day, lass."

"You, too, Mr. Martin." She waved as she crossed the street on her way to the secretarial position she had just begun.

It will be grand, she thought. William had for so long wanted to take his father from the poverty of the small village in southeastern Cork and had longed to see his younger brother and baby sister have a life he never had. William's mother had died from illness when his sister, Molly, was a child, and it pained him to know Molly was growing up without motherly affection. Katie had promised she would remedy that, even though the girl was almost an adult now. She would give the girl all the motherly love she would have given to her own two children had they survived the trauma of childbirth. She knew she was lucky to be alive, too. The births had been hard.

She thought of William standing over her and praying for her and the babies. It had been hard on him, and she recalled the promise he tearfully made God at her bedside that first time with their stillborn son:

"If yea let her live, I'll be about doin' anything I can to save other folks. I swear I will. And I'll share whatever goodness and light is given to me. Oh, God, do not forsake us."

William's Da wasn't well, Katie knew from the letters Molly had sent, and so there was more of an urgency in her husband's desire to free him from his land and obligations and to bring him to America. She was proud of William's strong resolve at putting money aside for his dreams. He had wanted to fulfill his ambition, buying out Mr. Dabney, the landowner and sheep buyer who had practically enslaved the O'Banyons and others for so long. William was determined to at least pay off the land and then bring his family to America.

William couldn't do any more for the village folks, his cousins, and others as he had always dreamed. But he was going to have a good talking to Mr. Dabney. His feelings were so strong against the landowner that she was worried that William might do more than just talk.

Being in the Merchant Marine gave him the right to go home at night when in port. Each month it meant spending up to a week at a time with Katie, just as he had promised before his ship, filled with war materials in New York harbor, would set sail for Great Britain or France once again. It was mid-October, exactly six months and as many crossings of the Atlantic before William's merchant ship, the *Othello,* made port in Dublin, Ireland, a layover before making its final destination, Liverpool. He had anxiously looked forward to the promise of one week in port there.

In four years of marriage, he had never met Katie's folks from Dublin. They had raised Katie and five other children behind their tailor's shop in a shopping district in the city. Billie made sure to bring gifts, a bottle of French wine purchased in Marseilles and two bolts of cloth sent from Katie in New York. They were the finest cotton patterns and prints Katie could find, impossible to get in Ireland.

William endured the day and night with his in-laws well, he thought. He was loving and kind to them, but his mind and heart were in County Cork to the south, a full twenty-four-hour train ride with stops. There it was his Da was lying ill, his brother, Phillip, a man of twenty now, and his baby sister, Molly, who he hadn't seen in eight years, would be waiting for him. He carried a roll of money—enough to pay off the note on his Da's small farm and bring them all to New York. It was in dollars, U.S. dollars, and he aimed to make a tight bargain with Mr. Dabney for the payoff. He had learned a few tricks of business himself and intended to use them.

Then, if he felt up to it, he would square off a good, solid blow to the round man's middle section and let him know of all the misery his family and others had endured because of him. If Dabney called the constable, no matter. He would be long gone, headed for Dublin with his Da and family. He'd simply board up the old homestead in Cork and come back after the war to improve it. With enough money, he and Katie could buy more land and become wool merchants themselves. Everything would be paid for with one-hundred-percent cash. He'd lend out at reasonable rates and gradually put old Dabney out of business. Then he'd buy the Dabney place, and his dreams would be fulfilled.

7

"M R. DABNEY will see you now," the butler announced as Billie paced anxiously in the foyer of the landlord's country estate. Billie had been waiting for this moment for as long as he could remember, at least since the last time he had been here as a lad accompanying his father on a visit to the ruthless aristocrat.

It wouldn't do for him to simply pay off the debts his folks had accrued. He wanted to face the land-and-wool pirate down—man to man—and if need be, rearrange some features on his arrogant and high and mighty face.

In his mind, he could still see the contemptuous sneer of the blue blood who had given a verbal drubbing to his poor tenant-farmer father when his Da came late with his land payments.

Only fifteen years old, he had wanted to tackle the landlord and soundly beat the stuffing out of him. They went hungry many nights for want because the high interest price the owner would exact would be almost more than they could bear. To buy food meant not paying the interest.

The rocky Irish soil only provided certain foods—potatoes, carrots, radishes. Watery potato-and-radish soup never satisfied. To eat a lamb was to eat future wool profits. They didn't starve, but they had been hungry. Too many times.

And as he had watched his Da grovel in front of old Dabney, begging him not to apply the late clause which would almost double the next year's payments, he had, for the first time in his life, thought that taking another man's life might be justified.

He had noticed his Da's clenched fists and beet-red face turn to little more than controlled rage as Dabney pulled out the contract and haughtily read the clause which would exact a toll so burdensome that Billie's Da wouldn't be able to afford feeding Billie and the two wee ones without taking an extra job. It was then that Billie had decided to find work enough to get him to America and help his Da, baby brother, and sister.

Now, Mr. Dabney's day had arrived, and he, William Robert O'Banyon, would deliver his Da's final due. He'd pluck his feathers one by one if the old codger started his lecture of how good he'd been to the O'Banyons and all the other kinfolk from town who "could not have made it without *his* generosity."

Billie confidently strolled down the voluminous and lengthy corridor leading to the study where, so long ago, he watched in agony as his father yielded to the financial whip applied by Dabney. *The hallways don't seem so huge now,* he thought.

A few more steps and he would settle this business, the matter that had consumed him for so many years, and then one day he'd come back from America to the family land. He and Katie would settle down with the land paid free-and-clear. With more money earned in America, he would create his own sheep business and go head to head with Dabney until he was out of business and out of people to filch. Then, for pennies on the dollar, he would buy out the old man and turn him into the street. These feelings might seem like hate to some, but to Billie it was simple justice.

William Robert O'Banyon would watch in satisfaction at the sight of the former land baron pleading for mercy. He would see Dabney and his children in the streets as beggars if he could. He needed just a few more good years, the bonus money from the Merchant Marine, and the war to last one more year.

Billie turned the corner of the hallway and passed by the courtyard. He noticed the flowering rhododendrons, the showy evergreen with white, pink, and purple buds. They were Katie's favorite. For such beauteous surroundings, the house was hollow, eerily cold, and quiet.

The butler announced Billie at the entrance to the massive library and study where an old man draped in bed covers coughed and wheezed from a chair situated behind a highly polished mahogany desk. His back was to the entrance where Billie stood.

"Mr. Dabney, I am William Robert O'Banyon of Kilgore. I'm here ta have a word with ye," Billie announced firmly.

"Mr. O'Banyon. Yes, yes. Do come in," the aged landlord coughed as he turned in his chair to greet him. "Robert's boy?"

"Aye."

"Do have a chair. Sit down, lad."

"I won't be stayin' long. I prefer to stand."

"Come now. Sit," the sickly Dabney urged.

"I've not come for sociality. I'm here on business." Billie hadn't expected a defenseless man of ill health. He expected the image from his boyhood—a tall man, proud, full of greedy energy.

"So ye are. So ye are," Dabney shook his head sadly. "Now let's see," he muttered opening the page of a ledger book. "Looks like you've been right timely with payments, and that, too, all the way from America. Good for you, lad."

Billie was caught off guard by Dabney's courtesies. His puffed up anger of fifteen years deflated. Dabney wasn't being nasty enough.

"No need to congratulate me for doing what any man would be doin'—takin' care of my Da and the wee ones. You'll be kind enough ta give me my payoff."

"I wonder what you expected of me, Master O'Banyon," the sick man mumbled through much effort in breathing. "Perhaps I should berate you? Belittle you perhaps? Snap my fingers, have men come, snatch your purse, and have ye thrown from my house?"

"What would ya be meaning by that, sir?"

"You're disappointed naturally. You expected a tall, proud, well-dressed man who would just as soon steal the land and watch ye starve as pay ye any mind."

"Aye. I recall such a man," Billie returned coldly.

"An' ye would've been just as happy to find me dead, rottin' in a grave, ta serve me right for all my evil deeds?"

"Aye."

"Well, you'll soon get your wish, lad." He coughed, violently spitting up into a receptacle beside his chair. "Thomas!" he called weakly.

The butler brought in a vial of liquid which calmed the old man once he drained it.

"Bring me the O'Banyon papers from Kilgore." He motioned with a listless hand gesture for Billie to sit.

"I am surprised, sir. I remember ye were my Da's age."

"Indeed, we may have been in age equal. But then you're father has not faired much better than old Dabney, now has he?"

"He has friends an' kin who love him. But aye, he has been sick. The tyrants of financial burden and time have taken their toll without mercy."

"Well spoken, lad. Do the tyrants rage no less against the rich man?" the landlord coughed.

"I wouldn't be knowin'."

"And what to show for it all?" Dabney spit back. "Robert has a fine, healthy lad respecting and honorin' him," he said pointing to Billie. "But me? Ah, for the love of the saints, I wish I'd been a poor man before seein' my lads fight each other over my estate. I'm a dead man already," Dabney moaned.

"I'm here to bargain for our land," Billie continued without show of sympathy.

"I am at the end of my path in life, lad. Even so, ye never knew me to bargain, have ye?"

"I'll make ye a fair offer," Billie returned.

The butler returned with the paperwork. The tired landlord reached shakily to the bundle and sorted through the papers. "I have a contract here that shows the principal sum of . . ." and he rattled off the amount. "Would that be correct, Master O'Banyon?" he wheezed.

"Aye. That, sir, would be the amount a usurious scoundrel would be seekin'."

Dabney roared at the remark—a mixture of coughed cackles. "I am sorry for my laughter, but I am in a melancholy mood, and I find my fate as a 'usurious scoundrel' a bit, well . . . a just indictment for the life I've lived, I suppose. I've never heard it put that way. Now, where were we? Ah, yes, the contract. Are ye a man of your word, Master O'Banyon?" he queried as he sipped from a steaming cup of tea.

"Aye. That I am," Billie answered.

"Then am I to expect the total principal due as stated in this document?"

"You have a right to," Billie shot back.

"But ye want to *bargain,* do ye?"

"I will pay ye a fair price in U.S. dollars," Billie revealed.

"I have a bank full of U.S. dollars. What is a U.S. dollar to a dyin' man, anyway?"

"More power and a right good bargain."

"For 535 English pounds, what is Master O'Banyon's dollar offer?"

"I'll give ye 420 and not a dollar more."

"Four hundred and twenty-five, and we have a deal."

Billie appeared stunned at Dabney's easy surrender.

The old man sneered. "You drove a hard bargain, lad. Now, out with the money before I change my mind."

"I'll be needin' the mortgage paper and a receipt."

"You think I'm daft?" Dabney barked. "Ah, your thick wool shearer's head wouldn't grasp the consequence of what I'm about to do if I explained it to ye in the clearest terms. Thomas, come here," he called to the butler. "You'll act as witness and count Master O'Banyon's money."

"Where do I see your signature saying I'll be gettin' my papers with land free-an'-clear?"

"Lay the money down, lad," Dabney growled. "You're tryin' this old man's patience."

Billie counted out the 425 dollars, handing them to Dabney. "The papers," he said.

"Aye, the papers and the receipt." Dabney signed the deed paid for in full with Thomas signing as witness. He scribbled in shaky cursive a receipt for the sum of 425 U.S. dollars and then said, "I'll be having ye sign a document of my own now."

"I'll not be signin' anything in this house. Nothing' good comes from it. I'm under no obligation."

"You'll be a fool if ye don't. I'm about ta make you an offer my own sons aren't worthy of."

"And why, sir, would ye do something to benefit me?"

"To spite the rascals waitin' for me ta die and because ya worked harder than any young man I've ever known. I respect that. Now listen, young Master O'Banyon, and listen ta me careful now," he coughed. "I'm not many days left in me. Look around. What do ye see?"

"Your estate, of course."

"Aye, my estate. My estate. Now, you sign these papers, and it will be Master William Robert O'Banyon's estate, and there is not a damn thing in the world my lads can do about it. If I haven't taught them to work in my life, by the saints, I'll teach them to work in my death."

"I do not know what ta think. I'm not sure what ye mean. You mean this land, this house, these properties will be mine? Why?"

"Are ye daft, man? I just told ye why! Sign here, now, an' make your decision quick before I have a change of heart," the ill man spoke in heavily breathed voice. "Thomas, bring me . . ." he spit up violently, begging for the mercy of the elixir Thomas ran for.

"I'll sign." The papers were laid before him. Billie read them quickly. He wished he understood the legalities, but he was smart enough to see that it was a deed and bill of sale. The sum of 425 U.S. dollars had been scribbled in as the amount.

He pulled his own mortgage papers from his coat pocket, for which he had just paid that sum, and found only "paid in full" beside the amount originally owed. This piece of paper certified his Da's debt was entirely paid.

He looked again at the scribbled receipt on the blank sheet of paper. It made mention only of payment to Dabney's entire estate.

Then he looked closer and read again: "The sum of 425 U.S. dollars paid in full for the purchase of the entire estate of Mr. Michael John Dabney."

"Excuse me, Mr. Dabney," Billie stammered nervously. "But this line here . . . does this mean you're given me your land, this house, and all ya have for 425 dollars? If ya are, I surely don't understand," Billie exclaimed apologetically.

"You don't have to understand it, Master O'Banyon. It's signed, witnessed by Thomas, and it's legal. Once I'm gone, you can fight it out with my sons. Do we have a deal or don't we?"

Stunned, Billie reached his trembling hand across the desk. "Its a deal!"

8

BILLIE SAT beside his father's weakened body knowing his dream of rescuing him, his teenage brother, Phillip, and fifteen-year-old Molly was all but accomplished. He looked sadly upon the once-strapping man he had known, feeling powerless about how to free him from the mortal fate so cruelly being dealt him.

"I cannot tell ye how glad I am ta see ya, laddie," Robert whispered with gravelly voice. "I thought the grim reaper would hew me down for sure before ye stood by me once again."

"I've never been away in my thoughts, Da. I came for ye. I paid the land off today. Dabney doesn't own us any more. Isn't that grand, Da?"

"Aye. Ya made me proud. A man couldn't ask for more than a son like my Billie. That's the dyin' truth."

"You'll be gettin' well now, won't ya, Da?"

"Ah, laddie. I've done my work." Robert O'Banyon stopped, gasping for air as his lungs gurgled with failure. "Look at ye," he continued with great effort. "Yer all grown up, a man now, and there's not a thing in the world stoppin' you three from havin' all ye want in life. Yer mother visited me a fortnight ago," he coughed. "Ah, she was a dream of a woman, she was." He began to shake with chills that suddenly swept through him. His eyes closed, and his mouth opened to gasp for air.

"It happens jus' like that, Billie," Phillip announced.

"I put more wood on the hearth, and he's colder. It doesn't seem ta do much good," Molly wept. "He's awake one minute, an' the next it's like he's out o' his mind with fever and ague."

"Da, I'll be holdin' ye till ya feel better," Billie gently offered as he scooped his frail father, blanket and all, in his arms and held him tightly against his own body to add warmth. "Don't go now, Da," he pleaded like a child. "We've got a whole lot a livin' ta do."

Perspiration beaded on the old man's face, and the chills left as suddenly as they came. It repeated itself in the same manner for hours as Billie faithfully held his once giant figure of a father in his arms.

Midnight came. Phillip added more logs to the stone hearth. Robert opened his eyes in a slow focus to see his son's face and smiled. "I was jus' dreamin' of ye, laddie."

"Was I a good boy in yer dreams, Da?"

He smiled weakly, "Aye, lad. *Always. Always,*" he whispered in barely audible tones. Robert's eyes grew large and opened in a fixed stare to the far upper corner of the room above the hearth where the warm fire blazed. He gasped for air, but his shaking eased to a stop.

"Da?" Billie asked, moving his face directly in front of his gaze.

Robert O'Banyon stared right through him. His mouth dropped open as if to speak. He gasped in a strained voice seeking words for the apparition before him, but air wheezed from the depths of his shallow lungs. He stared transfixed, wordless.

"Da, don't leave. Not now," Billie begged as moisture dropped from his cheeks and mixed with tears draining from his father's eyes.

Robert turned his head suddenly and looked into Billie's face and with struggling effort reached to stroke the boy's cheeks one more time. He smiled. "I love you," he said simply and closed his eyes without another breath.

"I love ye, too, Da. With all my soul an' heart I've always loved you. I'll make sure yer proud. By all the saints above, I swear I will."

They buried Robert next to their mother, Leah. Father Shannon officiated at the grave site. The entire village of Kilgore seemed to be there to honor the humble sheepherder and farmer they had known their entire lives. Few people ever escaped from the rugged life of Kilgore. Billie had.

" 'Twas a mighty fine wake and funeral, Billie," offered old man Collins.

"Thank ye, Mr. Collins. An' you too, Mrs. Floyd, Mr. Floyd."

"We're all sad at your Da's partin', Billie," Father Shannon offered as the last one to leave the hillside service. "I guess you'll be returnin' to America."

"Aye."

"Take this with ye, lad. Hang it on the wall and let it remind ye not of the death of our Lord but of his risin' up the third day. Let it remind ye that as the Father lifted his own

Son up, even so Christ will lift ye up to him, if you'll just ask him. Your Da knew it ta be true. If ye witness the light of the Son, his comin' from the grave, there will be no room for the darkness. We don't stay dead, lad. Be lifted up by the light . . . to Christ, laddie."

"I do not know if he will or won't lift me up, I feel so far down, Father."

"I know, son. It is one of the mysteries how he does it, but surely he will. It's his job ta do it, if you'll believe."

Billie's ship was setting sail from Cobh harbor to the north in twelve hours. He had left from there as a lad of twenty, almost ten years earlier, coming home to Ireland just twice in that time.

He gave Molly a tearful hug. "I'll be back with my Katie and our wee one by this time next year. I love ye, lass. Take care of the place and Phillip, too."

"I will, Billie. Please hurry home," she tearfully pleaded, burying herself in his massive embrace.

"I will. Now don't be cryin'. You know I will," he said with a kiss on her forehead.

"We'll be takin' over the Dabney place as soon as the old man passes. I figure his boys will be puttin' up a right good legal fight. Ye may be seein' papers from the county court. Heed them no mind. Pass the papers over to Squire Daniels. He'll be handlin' our affairs until I can return." Billie offered his hand to his younger brother, Phillip. Phillip threw himself into his brother's arms instead.

"I've missed ye, Billie. I surely have," he cried. "I want ta go with ya."

Billie swallowed hard. It was a pitiful sight to leave the two young ones alone.

"They say the war will soon be over now that America is in

it. I'll be finishing my obligation, and I'll be back. We'll never be separated again, you'll see," Billie said and broke free, picking up his bag and walking down the lane leading to the main village road and the highway.

"Write me, Billie," Molly called out in a muffled sob.

Billie turned one time to wave. He could barely make them out through the flood of tears staining his view. "Take care of our girl, Phillip."

"Aye. Ye can count on it, Billie," Phillip called back. Billie took his cap off and held it high over his head and waved.

9

ON NOVEMBER 11, 1918, World War 1 had come to an end and so had Billie's contract with the Merchant Marine. He was paid his bonuses, withdrew his savings from the bank, and was packed with Katie and his first-born son, Alexander, aboard the *Othello* as passengers. He was a working passenger, an arrangement made through his good contacts aboard ship. He had managed the cargo inventory well during his one and a half years with the ship as a Merchant Marine officer, and when he found they would be making a run to Dublin, he used his contacts to better his situation financially.

Billie wanted to conserve all the cash he could in order to start up the wool-trading and share-cropper business fairly with Dabney's former tenant farmers, his neighbors and friends.

Dabney had died two months earlier, and his sons had pursued their inheritance with a vengeance, but Squire Daniels, Billie's lawyer in Ireland, produced all the evidence the courts needed to dismiss the Dabney boys suit as "frivolous and without merit."

Billie's first act as landlord of the old Dabney estate was to call all the neighbors and kin who had dealings with Dabney and recalculate the debt. With the help of Squire Daniels, he restructured all debt owed the estate, forgiving some and making fair propositions to all the farmers, sheepmen, and property owners of the neighboring towns and villages.

Of course he made enemies, the Dabney boys among them, along with old business cronies who had burdened the people with exorbitant credit, making the folk of the surrounding townships and villages virtual slaves to their stores and places of business. There were threats of harm, but the loyalty of the village folk caused Billie, Katie, and Alexander to feel safe. Townsfolk and villagers alike regularly took turns guarding the estate day and night against the threats of burnings and livestock killings.

It was in late December 1918 when a killer arrived at the O'Banyon home that no one could have foreseen and none could have stopped from entering. The killer had spread its shadow across the European continent and even to the shores of America.

"Will he live, Doctor Muldoon?" Katie tearfully questioned as she leaned over little Alexander.

"He's mighty high in temperature. It's all in the hands of God, lass."

"In the hands of God!" Billie exclaimed. "The hands of God are in heaven. You are here. Do something for my lad, Doctor. Ye must. I'll pay ye any price, anything ye ask!"

"It isn't the money, lad. . . . If it were, I'd be wretchedly rich for all the folk dyin' this week an' offerin' me all they got. Right now the O'Malleys have lost their Johnnie, Mark, and now Sarah lies ill. Mrs. O'Malley, too. It's killin' whole families. Be grateful, lad, ye still got each other," the doctor said as he closed his bag and headed for the door.

"We thank ye, Doctor Muldoon. We are right grateful. Aren't we, William?" Katie offered with eyes brimming full of emotion.

Billie just looked away, out over the moors and far away to the sea where the waters carried the merchandise of nations back and forth—where he had lived and sacrificed twenty years of life to have what he had—a family, an estate, love, all that he could ever dream of. Now an intruder called the Spanish influenza was mocking his attempts to have his son grow up beside him and take over the O'Banyon name. It threatened his wife, his brother, and sister. Villagers were dying; Squire Daniels was ill and not expected to recover his full strength. The doctor said it did something to his heart. "Ah, God in Heaven, where are ya?" he moaned, head in hands.

"Ye asked him once before, remember? Remember, William, how he saved my life when ye prayed that prayer for me and the wee one we lost in New York? Pray it again, William," Katie urged, falling to her knees in reverence with William beside her.

"Dear Father in Heaven. I promised ye if ye would spare my Katie I'd be about yer business. Ye did spare her all those years ago. Now I know I promised I'd be about sparin' and savin' lives myself the rest of my days. I've been keepin' that promise. I want to bargain with ye. Give me my son to live. Spare me Alexander, and I'll give ye anything I have, includin' my life for all the rest of my days. I swear it in the name of the Holy One, Jesus. I will. Amen."

"And I'll give ye mine for his. Amen," Katie whispered.

"No, Katie. I couldn't bear it. What would ye have me do without you?" Billie said reaching for his young wife. They wept.

Standing, he went to his son and took him from the attending nurse. Holding him up to his cheek, he washed the perspiration gently with a damp cloth. "I love ya, laddie. I need you. Don't leave me now. We've got a whole lot of life left to live. We've got a name to build, a home, a destiny to live. Don't give up on us now."

Katie came and took Alexander to the rocker by the window. The full moon was setting against the Atlantic Ocean in the distance. She began to sing a lullaby. Little Alexander's breathing was labored.

Billie pulled up the sofa next to them to lay down. "Dear God, don't fail me."

When he awoke early at dawn the next day, Billie found Katie weeping. He threw off the covers and grabbed a listless and lifeless toddler from her arms. He stared, not knowing, not comprehending the moment.

"I don't know what happened! He was alive and gettin' better, wasn't he?" she cried. "Didn't God hear us? Oh, my baby! My darlin' little lad!" Katie fell to the bed embracing him. Moans of motherhood were carried on the still morning air.

Billie took the infant gently in his arms and placed him in his cradle. "I have not forsaken ye, God. Why have ye not heard?" he spit out angrily.

The next day Father Shannon arrived an hour before the graveside service. "I'm truly sorry for ye, William, Katie," he said embracing them. "The scourge seems to take the bright stars from us. He's with God now, and nothin' and no one can ever harm him, ever again."

"That's a small consolation, Father," Billie returned sarcastically.

"I know that it hurts, that you're full of sadness beyond any power my poor words can offer to comfort ya. Ye must believe and trust God, Billie. Yer lad is alive in Christ. He is, and a glorious meetin' awaits us all when this life of travail is done."

Billie looked at the priest, stupefied. "Words," he mumbled. His eyes were swollen red with rage.

"Father, will I truly see my darlin' wee one again?" Katie asked in throaty muffled tones.

"Aye. The Holy Book says, 'As in Adam all die, even so in Christ shall all be made alive.' Ye will surely hold him in yer arms again. Though the holy word doesn't say as much, I believe it."

"Then I must die to be with him?"

"We all must die at one time, only known to Almighty God, Katie."

"The townsfolk, how are they prosperin'?" Billie broke in.

"It's hittin' pretty hard, Billie. Not a home where someone hasn't died. I've never seen anything like it. I'm doin' one, sometimes two services a day. If I didn't have faith, I don't know what I'd do.

"The press says millions have died worldwide. Your U.S. newspapers that just arrived on the last boat to Cobh harbor say more U.S. soldiers have died from the Spanish flu than all the World War I combined. It says over 500,000 Americans have died and more dyin' everyday."

"I don't understand it. For the life of me, Father, I don't see why God is punishin' us. It's more than a man can bear.

I have given these people hope—for the first time in their lives someone is easin' the burden—and see how God has allowed it to be crushed out o' them?" Billie turned his back to the Father as the casket appeared on a carriage led by the stable hand, Jonathan.

"Thank ye, Jonathan. Be on yer way, lad. Take this home to yer Da and Mom." Billie handed him a small purse of coins.

"I'm truly sorry, Mr. O'Banyon. God knows I am. God bless ye, Mrs. O'Banyon. An' ye too, Father," the boy said backing away politely.

"God bless ya, son," Father Shannon added.

The service was a lonely one, attended by Katie and Billie alone. Phillip, Billie's brother, had been affected by the flu but not as violently as Molly. Billie asked Phillip to attend to his baby sister, expecting to see her when the service was done.

Billie opened the door of the old Dabney mansion to the sobbing cries of Phillip and knew that another dark night awaited him. He wasn't sure about God anymore, but he was sure about the devil. His baby sister, Molly, was dead.

10

BILLIE GAZED out in fixed stare toward the horizon as the passenger ship cut through the calm water off the coast of New England. He was a day out of New York harbor, and the horror had now taken a turn that was beyond comprehension.

His dreams no longer mattered. Nothing mattered. If he plunged into the sea and was swallowed by the largest fish in the ocean, would anyone notice? Who would care what happened to him? Phillip would, of course, but no one else. Because of his love for the sole surviving family member, he chose to live. But only for Phillip.

The insanity of all that had happened in the previous weeks was beyond his poor mind's capacity to analyze. Why had God chosen him to destroy? Why now? What if he had waited to go to Ireland? What if he hadn't taken Mr. Dabney up on his offer? What if he had left Alexander and Katie at home in America, calling for them later, much later? What if he had never met Katie?

"I am goin' mad!" he screamed to the setting sun from the railing of the top deck as he melted into a ball of uncontrollable weeping.

Sitting on the deck, head buried in his arms, he wanted desperately to turn back the clock twenty-four hours. "If only I'd been there. . . . If only, she had awakened me . . . to touch her soft face, a kiss. . . ." he groaned. The ship went on its way mocking his need for time to stand still. "My dear God, where is my Katie?" he sobbed aloud without shame. "Are ye real? Are ye there? Why have ye done this to me?"

No answer.

No one had seen Katie do it. She was ill; he was down with fever. She wandered out of their cabin while he was asleep. She walked out to the stern of the ship, and someone said they heard a cry, *"My baby!"* It was a woman's voice.

The deck hand who heard the scream went to investigate. He found no one on the deck at the stern. He dismissed the scream after turning his light onto the propeller-driven foaming water of the mighty passenger liner. No sign of a person. But then it was dusk. He failed to report the incident until the next watch. By then it was too late.

It was not until Billie awoke and realized Katie was missing from their cabin that he began to suspect something was terribly amiss. An hour after he had begun his search, he realized what awful depression had overcome Katie, and the force of what she must have done overwhelmed him. If death ever hurt, it couldn't compare with the breaking heart that was crushing life from him, from his deepest will to go on, to live.

The ship had been torn inside and out looking for her. Every cabin, the staterooms, the restaurants, bars, even the laundry rooms, boiler rooms, too—every space that could hide a living or dead human being had been searched with no trace of her.

Billie argued for the ship's captain to turn the ship about. The captain would not consider it. With no evidence that Mrs. O'Banyon had cast herself overboard in a fit of despair over the loss of her baby, other than the scream the deck hand had heard, the captain refused to attempt what would amount to "a futile rescue search at best," as he put it. The captain promised to pass a message along to the next ship following their route, asking them to keep eyes open for discovery of her body.

Billie walked to the stern of the ship and ran his hands all along the rail that Katie must have touched before her leap into the sea. It was here at this place now, a sacred place for him, where he would have to come to terms with what had happened.

Hadn't she loved him enough to consider what he would feel? How he would be destroyed? Of course she hadn't considered it. Her mind was full of despair, fever, and illness, too. She did love him though, didn't she?

Perhaps he could leave a note for Phillip. He could leave all his money, addresses of friends where Phillip could go to get a start in America. He was a strong boy. If he, Billie, could start in America without knowing a soul, so could Phillip with more of an advantage than he had begun with.

Phillip was lying ill in his cabin and had not yet been informed of the tragedy. When he awoke and was given the note, full of explanation, Phillip would understand why Billie had decided to join his wife, Katie.

Billie tearfully considered his options. He loved her. He couldn't live without her. He would die for her. If life hurt so much, then death could be sweet—if it meant to hold her, touch her, kiss her lips once more. He would be willing to go to hell for that—for just one kiss.

"Katie!" he screamed. "My God! Katie! Where are you?"

11

"ARE YOU still awake, Kathleen?" Peter O'Banyon asked his daughter.

She had nestled up against him. "I couldn't sleep, Dad. The story is so tragic. I wished I had known your Uncle Billie."

"He was a man's man, sweetheart," Peter softly whispered. "When I first told the full story to your mother, it was in a letter during the Second World War. She wondered what made Uncle Billie such a solitary man, yet so caring for others. It was then that we decided that if we had a daughter, we would name our baby Kathleen—"Katie," to honor Uncle Billie's wife.

"Did they ever find Katie's body?"

"That's a part of the tale that Uncle Billie wouldn't share. He would sigh and walk away the few times I dared to ask. But I have an understanding of Billie, more than any man could. . . . I've lived his life, you know."

"I know you have. I know," she sighed as she walked to the kitchen to pour a cup of coffee. "Dad, why are you so alert, so alive tonight?" she queried in a throaty voice. "I've missed you so much, and tonight it's like everything is okay; everything seems right; you suddenly don't have cancer; you're the old you." Katie fought back the tears as she poured herself the cup of watchfulness she would need this night. Parting with someone was never easy for her, but her father was taking the long path, a torturous exit that prolonged the agony she felt but also the joy in having him to talk to, to be with, to hold on to.

"Don't count me out yet. I've outwitted them doctors for two years now, you know."

"I didn't mean . . . Dad, you know what I mean," she said kissing him on the forehead and curling up next to him. "I wish tonight would never end. I feel like the little girl that used to live here in the fifties. I remember feeling so safe snuggled up here on the couch, you with the story books, the search light beaming out to the bay, the fire in the old potbelly stove. Aw, Dad, what's happened to people, to life? . . . Why can't it go on like that all the time?"

"Time is an obscure thing if one solely marks it by a calendar," he coughed. "It's made up of events and affairs of life, sweetheart. People make of time one occasion after another. The sum of life's events is how to measure," he smiled, coughing again. "Our time together counts far more than the clock of age that takes us from each other. Remember our time shared, sweetheart, and I will never be far away." His voice crackled with weakness, and his lungs heaved heavily at this effort. He reached for his daughter with moistened eyes. "I've loved all my time on earth, sweet Kathleen," he struggled again.

"Dad, here. Take a sip," she offered, bringing the hot liquid to his lips.

"Thank you, Kathleen darlin'," he smiled with a gleam in his eye as he settled back into his chair. "I guess you'd be wonderin' what became of my dear old Uncle Billie and why I carry this crumpled letter around with me?" Peter playfully broke into Irish brogue once more as he fumbled to find the logbook where the weathered letter marked his last entry.

"Here, Dad, I'll set it safely aside."

A deep seriousness overcame him as he reached for his daughter's hand. "It's important. That letter. You've never read it. Promise me, once I'm gone you'll keep it in my journals. It's all I have from him, from the lighthouse keeper," he implored.

"I promise, Dad," she responded stroking his tired face. "Get some sleep. We can finish the story in the morning."

"No. While the light shines out to sea, tonight, I have to finish. Am I too much trouble for you, sweetheart?" he asked, taking deeper breaths as the pain killers he had taken earlier wore away.

Katie shook her head and wiped at the tears staining her cheeks. She was a thoroughly trained hospice nurse. She sensed what was happening, yet it seemed that it shouldn't, couldn't be her own father going through this.

She helped him swallow water, and replaced his patch carrying measured amounts of morphine into his bloodstream. Kathleen suddenly realized how real the life and death struggle was for her ailing father. If this place hadn't meant so much to him, didn't do so much for him, she never would have allowed him to come so far from the care of the hospital.

"Am I a bother?" he whispered again.

"No, Dad," she replied somberly but with a smile, "I want tonight to last forever."

"Forever is a good place to start then. And the forever

in our family story is worth telling. Listen carefully, sweet-heart."

The flu epidemic of 1918 killed more than 25 million world-wide, they say. Between the war in Europe and the epidemic, there didn't seem to be a household which hadn't lost a loved one. One can become used to death, I suppose, but never can a loving mortal seem to shake the loss of the one he loved with all his heart. It was true for Uncle Billie.

Katie was everything to him. And I know what he felt when I say she was his soft breeze cooling the fevered brow, the gentle kiss of a spring dawn wisping through the fine laced curtains covering the window pane, the fragrance of every petal on a dew covered rose. Katie was his breath of life.

And the breath of life was like a blow, knocking the air from his lungs. He had moved his clothes from the bed and had knelt beside where she had lain. He needed to touch her some-how, and his feelings of abandonment by her and by God stirred him to curse and swear and break down in terrible feelings of guilt.

When he could not void another tear from his eyes, he reached for and lovingly began folding Katie's clothing to be packed away.

A gentle breeze brought a crumpled piece of writing paper drifting off the nightstand and onto the bed where he knelt. Written shakily in her delirium, Katie had left him a message he must have overlooked.

She wrote:

Dearest William,

Our Alexander has visited each night beggin' for me to come to him. I am so sick. My fevered mind asks, "should I go?" as he holds his hands out to me. He is my darlin' baby boy, and I cannot deny him. Yet my mind must be playin' tricks on me. Did we not leave him buried in Cork?

I see you near death dear, and maybe it is to be that we three shall always be together across the moor and fen to the land where no troubles or cares can deny our happiness.

I am confused. Will you leave me? I cannot awaken you. Has sickness taken you from me also? I cannot be without my two men.

I feel hot and must go up to the deck for air. If you read this note, come to me and bring a light, will you, love?

I love you with all my life and am afraid darlin' that you'll leave me behind. You're my light, my love. I'll be back soon. Come to me if ye awake before I do. I'm lookin' for our wee one.

Katie

Uncle Billie broke down. With this piece of love in his hand he knew that he would not now lose his mind. He at least had an answer for what compelled his beloved Katie to do what she did that fateful night, and now the burden of living in blame, guilt, and torture for not being able to save her left him as easily as a tiny down feather is lifted from one's hand and carried away on a breeze.

12

B ILLIE?" PHILLIP O'Banyon approached his older brother who sat staring blankly out the apartment window to the wharf below. "Billie? I need ta talk with ya," he said, breaking the silence that had enveloped the small room.

"Can't ya see I'm thinkin'?" Billie groused, biting down on an empty pipe.

"Aye and I'm sorry ta be botherin' ya, but I need ta tell ya somethin' that can't wait."

"Go on then," Billie answered without taking his eyes off the harbor scene.

"I've got me a girl, and we're plannin' to marry."

"Ya are, are ye?"

"Aye. Her name is Shannon Mulholland, and she comes from Galway."

"She's a Galway lass?"

"Aye, an' a right pretty one, too. Her Da has a dairy farm over in Jersey, and I've got myself some work all lined up, a small flat, too."

Billie turned to face the brother he had brought with him from Ireland six months before. "The warehouse ain't good enough for ya then?"

"It's not that Billie. I'm just not like you, what lovin' the sea like ya do. I love the land an' animals and working with my hands in the land. I'm a farmer, Billie, and I'm good at it."

"Aye. I know ya are. That I do know. We've still got land in Ireland. Have ye given it thought?"

"I plan to make enough to go back some day and never have my wife worry a day."

Billie's eyes were weary from sleeplessness. A wry smile crossed his face. "Dreams," he whispered, teeth still biting on his pipe. He turned back to the harbor.

"I'll be goin' at the end of the month."

"Do as ye please."

"I want yer blessin'."

"Ye have it."

"I need more than that Billie! Look at me!"

Billie turned to Phillip. "Go on."

"I need ta know yer with me and not sorry ya brought me to America. I know how ye miss Katie and the lad but we got ta go with life . . . what it brings to us. I want ya to be happy with my decision and . . . well, I jus' want ya ta be happy."

Billie stood and walked around the room, examining his slender, strong, handsome, twenty-year-old brother. "You've become a fine man, Phillip," he said approvingly. "I brought ya to America for yer happiness. If ya found it, then I am happy, too. God knows I am." He pulled his brother into his muscular arms. "I'm sorry I caused ya ta grieve. I'll be missin' ya."

"Ye could come, Billie," Phillip answered excitedly. "I've got it all figured out. There's room and . . ."

Billie held up his hand and waved it to silence Philip. "I'm a man of the sea. Ya had it right. The sea took my life from me, and I'll not leave it till I have her back."

Phillip began to protest.

"Shhh . . ." Billie motioned with a finger to his lips. "I'll have it my way, and we'll make a go of it . . . two O'Banyons, two paths to the same dream," he said, slapping Phillip on the back. "I'm glad for ya, Phillip."

"Katie!" He called out as he threw the covers off him. Billie sat up and shook his head and then placed his feet on the cold hardwood floor. *Another dream,* he thought. How close he had come to holding her this time though. Her arms were stretched out toward him, and he found himself running to her on the sea as if it were land. A bright beam had guided him, and at the moment of embrace she was gone.

Living without her was slowly killing him. He pulled himself from his bed and looked out to the beacon in the harbor, the small man-made island of rocks where a towering lighthouse stood guiding ships safely past it to the docks. *Maybe I should go back to Ireland, sell the Dabney place, and start working the family land,* he thought. *I have friends and kin there.*

He was lonely in a city teeming with people, immigrants, fortune seekers—constantly surrounded by people yet alone. He knew he should be able to start over. Katie had taught him how to talk to a woman, but any manly drive to look for someone else was gone. Every woman that passed by him on the streets reminded him of how he loved Katie still.

Billie dressed and reported to the docks early. He knocked

on the opened door to the warehouse office of his employer. "Mr. Pierce, may I have a word with ye?"

"Good morning, Billie. What can I do for you?" returned a man buried in his paperwork.

"Today will be my last day. I just wanted to thank you for all you've done for me and . . ."

"Sit down please, Billie," commanded Pierce in a business-like tone of voice. He looked up from his paperwork and handed a letter across the paper-strewn desk to Billie. "I've been expecting this. Frankly, you haven't been yourself, and I can understand why. We're all sorry about the loss of your family."

"What's this?" Billie asked, examining the envelope.

"Why don't you go ahead and open it?"

"I don't understand," Billie replied after examining the letter.

"I knew you couldn't stay here, Billie. I've been watching you. There are too many memories for you here. And believe me, I understand. I took the liberty to recommend you for a post with the New England Lighthouse Commission. A personal friend of mine is the commissioner. A new lighthouse sits on a small island—called Port Hope. It needs a keeper. This letter just came late yesterday."

"Why would ya think I'd find this attractive? All alone on an island off the coast?"

"Lighthouse keeping can be a lonely job, Billie. It takes a special person to do it. They look for good strong men who can dedicate themselves to the safety of the thousands of ships which pass along the coast to harbors here and elsewhere in New England. This is a real good offer, more money, free rent, a place to sort things out. When my friend Jeb Porter called and asked if I knew of anyone, I recommended you. Hope you don't mind."

"I don't know what to say," Billie stammered, his stinging red eyes seeking the composure of manhood. "I'm a lonely man, and no one will ever do but my Katie. I do need a change. Maybe . . ."

Pierce walked around from behind his desk and placed a hand on Billie's shoulder. "Give it a shot. Perhaps you'll find yourself out there."

Billie stood and shook hands with the warehouse owner. "You've always been fair with me. I won't be forgettin' it," he said.

"Good luck to you, Billie, and may you find the peace you're looking for."

13

UNCLE BILLIE'S decision to come here to Port Hope has forever made our family what it is. Without it, I never would have met your mother, never would have learned all the wonders that life has to offer. . . . Some decisions are simply more weighty than others. So it was with Uncle Billie becoming the first lighthouse keeper on this island.

"You know, Kathleen, I had the most marvelous daydream today out on the cliff. As I sat there, my mind went back in time, only it seemed more real than a dream. It swept before me in an instant but lingered in my mind for hours. Can I tell you about it?" he asked in a reflective voice.

"Uh . . . yes. Yes, Dad. Go ahead," she sniffled. Her gentle father was having a profoundly penetrating effect on her as he spoke in raspy tones, determined to spill out all that his life had meant to him. "I'll be right here listening, Dad," she finally offered with a quivering voice unintentionally revealing her brokenheartedness.

"Sweetheart. Are you sad?" he asked like a humbled child would to a parent.

"No . . . Yes . . . Dad, I don't want you to go," she cried softly, tenderly stroking his silvery hair, kissing his stubbled cheeks, trying desperately to maintain the strength he would need from her.

"Do my stories make it worse? I can. . . ."

"No. Oh no, Dad. Don't stop now. I want to hear all about you, Mom, and Uncle Billie. It's just hard thinking about . . . you know."

"That I'm dying?" he meekly said with a smile of satisfaction on his face.

"You don't need to be so cheerful about it, do you?"

"Oh, I'm not happy about the prospect of leaving you, but I am very content to see your tender feelings. Now I know you will keep close the things I'll share, the secrets of the lighthouse keeper, our legacy . . . I know you'll keep it alive. I can't help but be happy about that.

"You know, in my daydreaming state today, your mother was right there . . . today on the beach, like we were never separated. Odd, it seems like I was just nineteen yesterday," he said raising his crinkled age-spotted hands in front of him. "I daydreamed as I have a thousand times over the years that I stood there waving to her and then . . . it was 1942 again.

"Peter, you are the clumsiest, handsomest, silliest boy in all New England," Anna smiled as she slid down next to him. "Are you alright?"

Peter O'Banyon smiled back, slowly, unsure, and then examined himself. "I kind of lost it, didn't I?" he laughed.

"Kind of," she laughed.

"I used to be able to tumble down that sand dune under control. I don't know what's happening," he grinned. "Come on. What do you say we catch the breeze—go sailing for an hour?" he asked, grabbing Anna's hand and tugging her toward the small fishing pier and boat dock.

"Don't you love me?" she asked innocently.

"Yes," he laughed. "What's the matter?" he asked tenderly.

"You are acting like you want to avoid . . . you know. Today is special," she giggled.

"Oh, that! I love you. I still want to . . . you know," he whispered to her.

He glanced up the hill to the lighthouse. There was Uncle Billie, tinkering with the '37 Chevy. He waved to Peter with a wrench in his hand, said something, and then shuffled into the lighthouse. He should have told Uncle Billie sooner than he did about his and Anna's plans.

Peter followed Anna as she grabbed his hand and started to run toward the cove from the base of the sandy hill. He took in a deep breath of the salty air; the moisture from the wind-blown surf awakened his senses, and they splashed barefooted through the surf as they had a hundred times before when they were kids.

Running, they finally found themselves tumbling to the blanket Anna had laid out for them. A kiss, an embrace, and then Anna bolted up. "We eat first, right?"

"I'm not hungry," he said, nuzzling her neck with his lips.

"Chicken?" she asked happily as she opened the basket and fought his advances.

He could smell the freshly skillet-fried meat and the aroma of the baked rolls Anna always, so expertly, made for their Saturday picnics. This Saturday, however, was different. It was their last together, before he left for the induction center. Except that it was like so many Saturdays before—two carefree kids happy just to be alive and together on the windblown isle off Nantucket Sound.

He looked back again to the lighthouse that he shared with his Uncle Billie, the place he had called home since his parents died when he was a boy of ten.

"Sure. Chicken will be fine. White meat, please," he offered with a wide, toothy grin as he crossed his legs and sat, leaning back, staring at the girl he had loved for as long as he could remember. A permanent grin seemed to crease his lips, and she looked at him and wondered what he was thinking about. "I don't want to ever forget today," he said, taking in a deep breath of sea air. "I don't want to forget you," he voiced growing suddenly serious, taking in every line of her face, the deep sky-blue eyes that had teased him for so long, the slenderness of her shoulders, arms, legs.

"Peter, have some chicken before I start crying," she said as she slapped a drumstick in his hand. "I don't want this to end, either. Why now? Why did the war have to come along now?" she struggled. "Why didn't you tell me last week about your draft notice?"

He lay there silent, pondering the twist and turn of events that had overtaken him in the previous weeks, days. He was suddenly feeling sullen, trying to cope with the images that coursed through his mind, images of youth forever gone, images of leaving Anna.

"Peter. That's what's wrong, isn't it? You've been acting funny for days. Different. It's the fact that you are to report in four days to the induction center in Boston."

It was June 6, 1942. He stumbled on the words that followed as he tried to explain how he felt about doing his duty but not knowing how to handle her or Uncle Billie.

"I knew you'd have to go, Peter. Everyone is going to war. The world isn't standing still for us," she sighed. "I get cold thinking about the killing, about you leaving me for only God knows where," she shivered. "I do wish you had told me before now, though. I just don't feel prepared to say good-bye."

He stood up and walked towards the craggy outcrop of rocks that formed the breaker separating the cove from a wider, longer span of beach.

"Port Hope Island seems a million miles from Boston right now, and I feel like I just woke up from a long dream, growing up together, here with you on the island. I don't want that to end."

"We're still going through with it, aren't we?" she asked as she pulled him down into the warm, dry sand.

"You aren't afraid of becoming a widow?" he asked, intently gazing into her eyes for the answer.

"Don't talk like that. I don't want to think about the war. Not today. Kiss me."

They held each other for a long moment before Peter answered. "Yes. We're still going through with it."

"Hal's ferry boat leaves in four hours. What did you tell Uncle Billie?"

"Don't worry about Uncle Billie," he said, pulling her to him as he held her, and remembering meeting her for the first time here on this island.

14

To Peter O'Banyon, Anna was like a tiny toy magnet pulling iron from the sand. She had drawn him to her from the very beginning. The first time Peter saw her was in the summer of 1934. He was twelve years old. Uncle Billie had sent him down to the pier to work on the lobster traps and to see if they would be eating the bottom feeders for supper.

There were two ways down to the beach. One was the wooden plank stairs that switchbacked down, and the other was the sand dune. He liked the sand dune. With a good running start, Peter figured he could fly a good twenty-five feet. He had a pail in his hand and, without looking below, tossed it over the side then took a running start and leaped out over the edge and flew.

"Whahoo!" he screamed, flapping his arms as he went, pretending he was one of the gulls circling above him.

Landing, he hit heels first and then gravity added to his descent in a rolling head-over-heels motion until he came to the bottom of the hill. Rolling to a stop, he lay prostrate in the sand, happy to be alive.

And found he was not alone. He was looking up and into the most dazzling sky-blue eyes he had ever seen. She just stood there where he lay, smiling, then laughing, then running off toward the pier, crimson ponytails flopping up and down on her shoulders. The cutoff trousers and midriff blouse tied in a knot revealed a fair-skinned girl probably not accustomed to the summer sun's coloring power.

Beet red. She'll be burnt to a crisp by the end of the day, he thought, picking up his pail and following her.

"Hi," Peter announced as he reached the end of the pier where she sat, dangling her feet in the water. "Lots of sharks in the bay," he added simply as he began to tug on the lobster-trap ropes.

"Ahh!" she squealed, pulling her feet out suddenly from the cold water.

He laughed.

"What's so funny?" she demanded.

"I dunno. Maybe you've never been shark bait before."

"It's not funny."

"You laughed at me first."

"I did not."

"You did so . . . over at the hill."

"Humph! Well then, we're even."

"Guess so."

"What's your name?" she boldly questioned.

Peter pondered on his answer as he tugged on the ropes. His heart was beating faster than it did after a race or a swim across the small inlet cove. "That depends," he said.

"Depends on what?"

"Depends on what you want to know about me."

"Okay. Do you live on the island?" she asked.

"Yep."

"Do you live near here?"

"Yep."

"Do you live here only in the summer or all year round?"

"From January to June on the weekends. September to December, too."

"And?" she prompted.

"And all summer long," he smiled. She was so cute. His heart continued to pump as rapidly as his tugging on the rope.

"What's your name?"

"You're the new one on the island, right?"

"So?"

"You tell me your name first," Peter demanded as he grabbed the lobster trap out of the water.

"Anna. It's Anna Weatherby. What's that inside?"

"You're kidding me, right?"

"Don't make fun of me. Just tell me."

"It's dinner," he smiled. "I've got to be going. My uncle's waiting up at the lighthouse."

"You never said your name," she followed.

"Pete. Peter O'Banyon. See ya tomorrow."

"I gotta go home, too. Can I come and see the lighthouse on my way home?" she asked tagging along after him.

"Sure."

They walked up the stairs, her mouth going full blast, blurting out her whole life it seemed. Peter wondered if she was that way with everyone she met or just trying to make up for looking silly about the shark-bait stuff and not knowing what a lobster was. He grinned. She was darn cute.

. . .

Peter O'Banyon had shared his family history with an unnatural energy . . . not earthly, or so it seemed to Kathleen who had listened in silence for more than an hour as her father endowed her with his life story.

He had given her knowledge of a kind people do who desperately seek remembrance, people who seemingly have one foot beyond mortality yet retain a capacity to utter reverent things, sacred to those whose blood lines will follow them into eternity.

She gazed to sea in a fixed state of ponderous quiet as he relaxed in the easy chair, conscious of her meditative contemplations.

"I never knew Mom, not really. . . ." Kathleen finally said, breaking the thick silence. "You've been in love with her like a school boy. All these years, I never understood. I understand now," she offered wistfully. She swept a gentle hand across her father's wrinkled brow and ended her reflections with a kiss.

He smiled.

She walked to the kitchen, poured a cup of coffee, then sipped it while looking out beyond the small inlet and cove so brimming with the life her mother and father had together. *Who would have known a love story could happen to two people so distant from the real world, so isolated,* she pondered. She had never seen her father as a sophisticated man, a man of great knowledge, though he had taught school and had written articles for the *Northsound Gazette* published on the mainland.

Why had it taken so long to understand him, she wondered with an audible sigh of tension-filled breath releasing from her lips. She looked back at him, cancer-ridden but relaxed as if he had almost finished his accountability marking his seven-decade-plus existence.

A love like this, love of life and all it has been, needed to be shouted to the world, she thought. But then what does a young person know until five decades later, as she now had herself lived. Age, life, history, family . . . it meant something to him. To watch him slowly die sealed the meaning for her in a way she never could have known.

Kathleen walked back to the lighthouse keeper and sat by his side once more. "Tell me more, Da—will ya?" she smiled with watery eyes.

"Aye," he coughed with a pleasantness in spite of it. "You are feeling the words. That's good. You won't forget . . . now I'm sure." He began again to tell the story that had made it possible for him to be called a "lighthouse keeper."

15

HELLO, LAD," Uncle Billie said somberly, shuffling his feet from side to side.

"Hello, Uncle Billie." Anna held onto Peter's arm.

"So, ya are makin' yer love a legal matter are ya?"

"Aye," Peter laughed, a hint of embarrassment in his feigned Irish accent.

"Well then, I must be givin' ya this. Your mom wanted you to have it. Jus' before she died, she whispered ta give it ta ya when ye were all grown up. It isn't much, but it meant somethin' to her. Her beau gave it to her—your Da—on their weddin' day. Best look at it and do the proper thing, lad."

Peter reached out for the locket. He opened it to see the picture of his young parents, Phillip O'Banyon and Shannon. Etched in the silver on the opposite side were the words: *"I swear by all the lights in heaven above, forever and ever you are my love."*

Uncle Billie just nodded, eyes glistening proud. "Do what

you must, lad." He knew they couldn't afford a ring. Uncle Billie flicked his hand towards Anna to prompt Peter.

"Anna?" Peter motioned her to come to him. He undid the chain and then put it around her neck. "I swear by all the lights in heaven above . . ." He couldn't finish it. His thoughts mixed with the emotions of leaving the man who had raised him like a son, the images of his parents—faint now—and the tragedy that had taken them so many years before.

Anna stroked the solitary tear on his face and held him tightly to her. . . . "Forever and ever you are my love," she whispered as she held him. Peter rested his head on her shoulder, and the fears and memory of the tragedy that brought him to Port Hope Island rushed through his mind with lightening speed. The locket he hadn't seen for so many years brought them back.

"Peter? Are you okay?" Anna posed tenderly.

He raised himself up from her shoulder, vision broken, and answered. "I've never been better, darlin'." He held her head in his hands, kissed her tenderly, then turned to his uncle, now bent with age.

He looked into Billie's eyes and saw the man who had rescued him; who had taken his hand at the grave sites of his parents and gave him a home and taught him everything he guessed he understood about life, God, and things a man should know.

"Be a good lightkeeper, lad. Make me proud," the old man choked as he offered his parting advice. "I been meanin' to say . . . well, I love ya, lad."

Peter pulled his aged Uncle to him. "I love you, too, Uncle Billie. I'll do my best to remember everything you taught me in this place—every single thing a lighthouse keeper should remember," Peter smiled, swallowing back salty moisture. "I'll make you proud of me, I promise."

"I already am, lad," Uncle Billie said as he stood back admiring his work. "My dear God . . . you are a man, aren't ya?"

Anna came forward and gave Uncle Billie a farewell kiss on the cheek.

"You'd better be off now. The ferryboat won't wait all day."

Peter simply nodded and gave his Uncle a final manly embrace and then took Anna's hand to leave. As they walked down the path, Peter tried to take it all in. The place that had changed his life, had become every part of him—he might never see it again.

Peter and Anna reached the path leading down to the beach and the pier and looked back one final time.

"Give 'em hell, boy. I'll light the lamp each night for you, . . . son." Uncle Billie waved and turned slowly, hiding his broken composure in the safety of the lighthouse.

Peter waved and drank in the sight of the round pillarlike home guarding Port Hope Island and offering those seeking safety their harbor from stormy seas. Maybe the light would be there for him . . . bringing him home again.

"I want you to have this," Anna cried softly. "It'll remind you of our four days and nights together."

Peter tried to be strong for her—for them both. He stuffed the padded package with the letter Anna handed him in his handbag as the Greyhound bus pulled into the station.

"I'm not sure what I'm supposed to say, Anna," he said, seeking an even unbroken voice. "Hey! Look around us. Just a bunch of sobbing crybabies going to war," he whispered to her as she pulled his head down to hers.

Couples were kissing and embracing as the new draftees

started gathering closer to the bus that was to take them in to the Boston induction center.

"They'll probably give us a leave, you know. Anyway, we have to be shipping out from New York, once we're trained, at least if they send us off to fight the Nazis. I'm sure we'll see each other again, maybe have a night or two together, before heading overseas. Who knows, maybe I'll still stay in the States or something," he tried to cheerfully reassure Anna.

She wasn't buying it.

"Guess this is it. I'll write as soon as I find out where they're sending us. I love you," Peter called from the first step of the bus.

"I love you, too, darling," Anna mouthed as she blew him a kiss with a vain attempt to smile.

Peter moved down the aisle to the back seat on the bus where he could watch the station as the bus pulled away. Anna saw him, and they held up hands to each other as the bus began to roll.

She ran out into the street and after the bus, then stopped and screamed, hoping he could hear her.

"There's a lighthouse waiting for you! I love you, Peter O'Banyon."

"I love you, too, Anna O'Banyon. I love you, too," he mouthed in return.

The bus ride took two hours. It was midday by the time they arrived at the old courthouse downtown. Growling Army master sergeants held clipboards in their hands and bellowed out names as the men got off the bus, ordering them to "fall in line" by last name.

"O'Banyon! To the right," a sergeant called out.

Peter responded by getting in line on the right.

"Hey, mac," called a new recruit from the left line. "Hey, you," he called looking at Peter.

"Got any idea which line is best?"

"They say the left line is the air corps," Peter called back.

"Hey, man, I'll trade you. I don't like heights so much," the shaky-looking recruit offered.

"I'll take my chances here. Thanks anyway," Peter returned. The processing began and within four hours Peter O'Banyon was weighed, probed, pushed, and prodded, then classified "1A" fit for combat duty.

"How come everybody is classified 1A?" one of the new recruits grumbled as they sat outside the courthouse, awaiting instructions.

"Yeah. That guy over there? Look at him. He couldn't see two feet in front of him without them Coke bottle glasses. That guy over there? A good breeze would knock him over."

The small group of men laughed.

"Hey, pal, my named is Joey. Joey Cipriano. I play poker, blackjack, and craps. You like craps?" he asked as he pulled out some dice from a shirt pocket.

"I dunno," Peter replied, staring off towards the harbor. "Never done it."

"Hey look, this guy's got some dice," another draftee blurted out. Soon, a small group of ten men created a circle and the rolling began.

Cipriano rolled one final time. "Come on, lucky seven. I need ya, baby," he said, kissing the dice and then throwing them into the circle. "Whoo!" he yelled, pulling in the cash scattered on the ground.

"Let me see them dice," grumbled one of them.

"My pleasure," Joey smiled with a little bow as he handed them over.

"Don't be such a sore head. They call it *craps* for a reason," mumbled another draftee with a smirk.

"Hey, Pete. That's your name, ain't it? Come on over here. Look at this wad of cash, will ya? There must be a hundred dollars here easy. Man, the Army can't be all bad," he laughed, kissing the money. "Here," he said throwing a five dollar bill at Peter.

"Ah, no thanks. I lost it fair and square."

"Hey, man. You turning down Joey Cipriano? It's bad luck to turn down Joey Cipriano. That's your 'lucky five.' You use that five-dollar bill each time we do craps and you'll be a winner. I'll teach ya everything ya need to know," the cocky and taller Italian-American said pulling Peter under his arm.

"Thanks, Joey," Peter grinned back.

"Here we go again," Joey offered as a sergeant approached the group.

"Lines," Peter grinned back.

"Yeah, lines. Long beautiful lines full of dumb suckers willing to lose their dough," Joey laughed.

Peter pulled the letter out of his handbag, the one Anna had given him earlier that morning. He handled the soft fabric in the package. It was beautiful, a reminder of why he had to make it back. And a War Diary—brown, leather bound with brass clasp—the size that fit easily into the palm of the hand. Anna asked him to fill it with his experiences.

Peter had read the letter a couple times on the bus, but he had wanted to read her words again now. They had a flavor, a taste, as sweet as her mouth when they kissed. When she wrote to him, everything poured out of her, and the words brought her to life in his mind. He wasn't too good with words and wasn't sure why she had ever liked him in the first place, but he was a lucky man—far luckier than Joey Cipriano. She had given him everything she had, and he wasn't going to let the Army, a German or Jap bullet or bomb take that away from him. He read the letter again:

My darling,

I had a friend take this picture of me down by the pier a couple weeks ago when you had gone with Uncle Billie for lighthouse supplies. I wanted several shots of me in my bathing suit so that I could send you the best one.

Some of the girls say the English women all work our GI's over pretty good so they can come back with them to the States when this is all over. Others say the English women are the prettiest on earth, and that when we send our boys over there, we don't stand a chance.

I'll bet none of them have a bathing suit like mine and just the right location to wear it. So if you ever get tempted, I hope these photos send you a message.

I'm waiting. So is the lighthouse. Uncle Billie and I will be shining the light for you everyday, sweetheart. I feel like the luckiest girl on earth. I love you, darling. I pray for you everyday. I'm so glad I'm your wife.

Anna

16

As she allowed Uncle Billie to serve her dinner, Anna toyed with the wedding dress she had worn just four days earlier. Uncle Billie was the kindest older man she had ever met. A little quiet, like Peter, but every bit of him was kind.

"Here ya go, love," the aging Irish seafarer said handing her a hot plate of beef stew.

"Thank you," she smiled.

"You're welcome, darlin'," he nodded as he returned to the small kitchenette and poured two cups of tea, one for her and one for him.

"It's sure nice to have a woman here . . . again," he offered wistfully, sitting next to her in the worn-cushioned armchair.

"Peter never said there had been a woman living here before," Anna answered with a questioning gaze.

"Well, I only imagined her, I guess. Maybe I never told Peter as much as I should've," he mumbled and then got up to put some of his stew in the dish for his old sheepdog. "Here ya go, boy," he said, patting his dog on the head as the animal licked tentatively at the still warm porridge.

"I'd love to hear about her," Anna prodded.

"It still brings me a wee bit o' pain . . . so I don't say much," he answered politely, shuffling back to his chair. "Ya must a looked beautiful in that gown of yers," he pointed, avoiding Anna's questioning.

"Would you like to see me in it?" she asked.

"Aye. It'd be balm on an old man's eyes to see ya in it, lass. But it would never do without Peter here." He got up and walked to the bay window and looked out to the distant hazy blue line across the ocean horizon. "It's been too long without a real lady in the lighthouse," he whispered in low voice. "Oh, there's never been a lady here . . . I imagine her, but she's not real . . . not really here," his voice fell off.

Anna got up and held the dress against her, wanting to brighten up the old man. "I always wanted a big wedding with lots of people staring and 'oohing' at my gown . . . like they would a princess, you know."

"Aye, and yer every bit of that, darlin'," Uncle Billie laughed.

"You can be our best man, and I'll pretend to be walking down the aisle with Peter. Wait right here." Anna excitedly ran to the small bedroom, just off the kitchen, an old storage room Uncle Billie converted for her and Peter.

Uncle Billie looked out over the bay and sighed. He couldn't spoil her childlike joy. He struggled for composure. It still hurt, like it was yesterday, not twenty-three years ago.

He had never told Peter of his young wife's fate. He had referred to her simply as Mrs. O'Banyon. "When Mrs. O'Banyon was still alive . . ." he would begin and then with a tidbit here and a tad of information there Peter had learned something about Uncle Billie's love. Now, this young woman was bringing it all back to him as if time was never past, never future, but everything present. He wasn't nearing his sixties in his mind, nor in his heart. He was young, strong, and very much in love.

How could he now divulge to Peter's wife his own love's story without falling into a deep, uncontrollable sorrow? How could he tell her what had happened on a stormy night in January 1919? They were young marrieds and recently given the whole world only to have it dashed to pieces by the scourge that plagued the earth like the devil himself had taken over. There had seemed no justice in it.

He would like to tell her how the lighthouse changed all that, the feeling of despair and ruin. He would tell her just to reflect and find a validation in his ideas about his service on Port Hope Island. He wanted her and Peter to know what he had planned for them and the lighthouse once he was gone. The doctors had warned him of his failing lungs, that he should have someone to help him and watch out for him.

Had an angel sent Anna to Peter and him to bring some joy back into a life so cruelly treated? He thought about Anna and her perky spirit and chuckled. She was Peter's "Katie." He would see to it that they had a fine inheritance and a long life, God willing.

"Katie," he whispered, looking out to the bay as Peter's young wife returned.

"Uncle Billie? How do I look?" Anna asked as she modeled her wedding gown for him.

"Aw, Anna darlin'. Ye look so mighty fine. So very mighty fine." He sighed, aware that he had slipped temporarily into the past.

"Peter and I wanted a big reception, like those you see in

the society columns, but I'm not disappointed. He said after the war he'll come back, and we'll repeat our vows in a garden over in Hartford at my parents' home. Will you come, Uncle Billie?"

"Aye, lass. That I will. I wouldn't miss it for the world. Did your parents fuss much about you and Peter eloping?"

"A *wee* bit," Anna grinned.

They both laughed. *It is so good to laugh,* Billie thought. This young women was giving him a piece of life and heart he hadn't known for over twenty years.

He turned the dark-oak Silvertone table radio on and tuned to Boston's *CBS Sunday Evening with the Philharmonic Orchestra.*

"I used to dance long ago," Uncle Billie offered, holding out his hands meekly to Anna.

"I'll bet you were quite the charmer at each Saturday night ball," Anna said walking toward him.

He stammered as he shook his head gently. "If ya would do me the honor, it would be grand ta try again."

"You know the waltz?" Anna asked cheerily.

"Aye . . . but I did a jig much better. I'm not sure my heart nor my back could take a jig ever again. But, aye, I did learn the waltz once long ago in another's arms. I'd be obliged greatly if ye counted out the steps." His moist eyes glistened in a hopeful way. He was going back to Katie in his mind.

"Now, here's how we'll start," Anna said holding his hands in a waltz position. "I'll begin the count. One, two, three . . . one, two, three . . ."

17

ANNA KISSED Uncle Billie good-bye. She had to hurry and catch the ferry for Nantucket. From Nantucket the ferry would take her to Boston, then to her Connecticut home. With summer gone and pleasantly spent, helping both Uncle Billie and her parents who ran the small general store, during the vacation months she would go spend the fall and winter in Hartford.

She loved the lighthouse, and the warmth of the evenings spent gazing out into the vast shimmering sea. The lighthouse beacon made it shimmer, sometimes glisten. Then adding the expanse of stars at night and a full moon it reminded her of endlessness, eternal possibilities . . . of life.

The ocean gave life, she thought. It seemed her friend, a comfort. Even on stormy days she could see the beauty in the rage of the currents: swirling, churning, making something new out of the shoreline, and reminding her that life was like that.

Stormy.

Then calm.

Followed by beautiful vistas of blue.

And billowing clouds of gray . . . trouble.

Returning to clear and brilliant skies, gentle breezes, and soft sounds of foamy breakers healing the beach with a sweeping caress.

And the lighthouse was always there. Through good days and bad, it stood magnificently strong, doing what it did so well: giving light by night and standing sentinel by day to serve the seafarer.

And pleasure. It gave immense pleasure to the eye of anyone on their journey near the isle because it fit. It fit on the hill like a master controlling the events created by the elements of nature surging around it.

To Anna, nothing could be more manly and nothing more romantic than the thought of Peter, the lighthouse, and endless dreamy days of peace surrounded by the powerful Atlantic. He was her painter, the island the canvas, and she the goddess of all the love made there.

War spoiled the dream for now. But she would come back to wait and keep watch with Uncle Billie. As fearful as she felt for Peter's safety at war, she knew deep inside they were destined to live and love here. Peter would be back. She was certain.

Now, she had to go and wait. When he finished his basic training, they would have perhaps a day or two, and she would never let him forget it.

Like the gentle, foamy breakers stroking the sand with lapping motions across its silver strands, caressing the shore tenderly, they would some day, too. *That is the reward after the storm,* she thought. *To enjoy gentle caressing, in waves, over and over again.*

. . .

Grand Central Station was a sea of men in uniform making connections to other trains and passengers wending their way home from a busy workday in New York City. The war accentuated the business of the place, moving people to a hundred locations daily without the slightest trouble.

And the war added new life and zest to the station. Not such a cold and endlessly somber business as usual, there now seemed an excitement, a strange pulse-like beat that the distraction of wartime seemed to offer.

Then there was the desperation found in servicemen seeking out their sweethearts and girls squealing with joy to see someone they longed for, now in uniform, spinning them around, twirling them with anticipation of the day or two they would spend together. Anna had rented a hotel room for two nights. She was determined to make the time spent with her husband something he wouldn't, couldn't forget.

She knew she should be grateful. Peter could have easily been shipped to the West Coast or Midwest for training and then straight to the Pacific where all the fighting was going on. She looked for reasons to be grateful. She knew her situation was exactly the same as a million other wives, maybe even better.

Now, she must be patient. They had agreed to meet in the central lobby under the huge, electronic message board flashing the latest news from the battle fronts. But it was impossible to wait hour after hour without doing something, anything. So she walked from gate to gate, questioning each ticket attendant for news of inbound trains with any possible connections from Kentucky.

It was entirely possible that she had made a mistake. After all, Peter's letter was so sketchy. He had sent her a "V-mail" and it had been brief. She tapped her watch. It was getting late, nearly 6:00 P.M. There was a bench across from the flashing message board overhead. Another young woman had just found whom she was looking for and had flung herself at a sailor passing by. Anna quickly took the seat and waited.

Time passed so slowly when one wanted something desperately. Like a child waiting for her birthday or anticipating the joys of Christmas, she couldn't speed up the appointed arrival of her gift—Peter. She was so anxious to feel his arms hold her in safety that she imagined his voice in every one she overheard.

Although the trains, their sounds, the boarding calls, the happy families greeting soldiers, mocked her attempts to discern one voice over another, she imagined she heard Peter's in the group of soldiers entering the large Grand Central Station lobby.

It couldn't be. They were loud. The raucous group of soldiers squeezed past her and throngs of others continually moved in and out, making the place a jumbled mass of bodies. She would have to stand on the bench just to make out a familiar face. Peter was more subdued, not loud as these soldiers where, but then again their backs were to her, and she thought she recognized one of the voices.

She knew she had been imagining his voice all day, and she knew she was growing tired, but just in case, she decided to stand above the gathered crowd and look out to see if it could be him.

She took off her high heels, holding them in her hand, and stood on the parklike bench, eagerly searching for Peter's face among the throng of soldiers gathering nearby. They seemed to be saying their parting farewells. She strained to hear their voices as she arched back, looking over at them.

One soldier caught her attention. He was loud, obviously happy, maybe six feet tall, with dark wavy hair, using hand gestures to make his point, and talking to a slightly shorter but muscular-looking soldier with his back to her. The less-excited soldier seemed to be checking the electronic message board with a certain ambivalence to what the other soldier was saying.

"Like I told ya," he said, "you bring the little lady down to Jersey, see. Mama will feed ya the best pasta on the East Coast, see. And Papa, he'll just sit there with a glass of wine in his hand, sayin' nothin'. And you two can have the apartment next door, free of charge, for two whole days. What ya say?"

Anna jumped off the bench, shoes in hand, and moved excitedly through the crowd. She couldn't be sure since the quiet soldier stood a good two inches shorter than the taller, dark-haired one doing all the talking. She had never seen Peter in uniform, but she knew his back, his shoulders, the way he stood, relaxing one leg over the other.

"Peter?" she called out timidly.

The soldier turned with hopeful eyes.

"Peter!" Anna ran into his arms as he dropped his duffle bag to his side. "Peter, I love you. Oh, Peter, hold me," she cried, softly burying her head against him.

"Anna, darling. I've missed you so much." He smothered her in his arms and kissed her anxious lips.

"Uh humm," the other soldier cleared his throat.

"Oh, yeah. Anna I want you to meet a friend of mine. Anna, this is Private First Class Joey Cipriano, the crazy Italian tank driver I've been telling you about in letters," Peter jabbed.

"Not too crazy to know a beautiful woman when I see one," he smiled and took off his service cap respectfully. Taking her hand, he said, "Peter, she's too good for you." Then kissing

Anna's hand he continued, "Now I know why you won't come down to Jersey to try Mama's cooking. I wouldn't either. It's a pleasure to meet you, Anna," he added suavely.

"You're sweet," Anna blushed.

"And you deserve better. But maybe you can make something out of this guy. I can't seem to get him to enjoy life. Maybe you can. Hey, see ya in a couple days, pal," Joey slapped Peter as he turned to go. "Don't be doin' anything I would do," he laughed as he disappeared into the crowd.

18

PETER'S TIME with Anna was a short-lived, blissful few days. Almost as soon as he kissed her hello, they were clinging to each other saying good-bye. The furlough after basic training was too short.

Peter had peered out the train's window, rain streaking across it, sitting in silence and agony as he traveled with his army buddies back to Fort Knox, Kentucky, for combat training.

Arriving late in the afternoon, Joey threw his bags on his bunk and pulled Peter aside. "Hey, Pete. What ya say we hit the town tonight?" Joey said, rubbing his thumb and index finger together on their first weekend pass after arriving. "The big three "B's" tonight . . . I'm feeling lucky."

"Three B's?" Peter asked with a smile but no interest.

"Broads, booze, and bucks," Joey grinned. "Come on, I need my lucky Pete O'Banyon with me. I've won since the first time we met . . . remember?"

"No, thanks, Joey. You go ahead. I've got some writing to do."

"Hey, man. You got to loosen up. This is Fort Knox, Kentucky; home of the mighty First Armored Division. We're tank jockeys, and I got this lucky feeling about tonight," Joey urged. "Hey, Pete, if it's money, no sweat. I'll cover for ya. We'll go throw some dice, rob a few infantrymen, and then hit a bar or two. Come on, man. You're my lucky charm."

"Joey, your makin' me feel guilty. But I can't. I got to finish this letter to Anna. I don't write so good. It takes me a lot of thinkin'. But you go ahead and have a good time."

Joey wouldn't let up. Peter finally rose from his bunk and walked towards his tall, obnoxious Army pal and dipped his shoulder into him.

"Hey, man, put me down. What you doin' trying to embarrass me?" Joey asked, ruffled as he freed himself. "I'm bigger than you. These guys won't let me live it down."

"If I have to embarrass you so you'll leave me alone about goin' out, then I guess I will."

They stared each other down until Joey couldn't take it any longer and burst out with a loud roar. "You know why you're my lucky charm?" Joey asked, slapping his friend on the back.

"No, why?" Peter asked as he returned to his bunk.

"Because you're the only one of these slobs who does what he says he'll do. . . . You keep your word to your wife. I can trust a man like you. You'd make my Papa proud if you were one of his sons. You're like the brother I never had. I mean it, Pete. You're as steady as a rock."

"Thanks, Joey," Peter returned. "I'm your pal, brother, and will stay your 'lucky charm.' Just stay out of trouble, will ya? I don't want to have to bail you out somewhere."

As soon as Joey had left the barracks, Peter reached into his footlocker and pulled out the package Anna had given him ten weeks before. He found the letter and put it to one side. Then he unwrapped the pillowcase. The other soldiers in his platoon would make fun of him, if they ever saw it, but when he could, he wanted to lay his head down on it and smell the perfume that Anna wore. She had soaked it in the fragrance. The pillowcase had their names embroidered: "Mr. & Mrs. Peter O'Banyon. Married June 6, 1942. Nantucket, Mass. *Forever and ever you are my love."* Cherished words from the family heirloom, the locket Peter had given her instead of a ring, were stitched there and also were deeply imbedded inside his heart.

Anna had purchased a small War Diary for him. He wasn't much of a writer, but she asked him to keep all of his war experiences in it. He kept it in the pillowcase and wrote a line or two each day. Army life was so boring and at times so mindless. They taught him how to destroy things and kill people. That's what armies do. What was he supposed to write about then?

He looked at the light-brown leather diary with a brass latch, opened to the day, and simply wrote, "Thinking of you, darling. That's all." Then he set it aside and held the satin pillowslip in his hand. He longed to lay his head beside hers again.

An embroidered replica of the lighthouse and the hill looking out to the bay was elegantly and carefully handcrafted by Anna. He wanted to feel each stitch because her hand had been there. He used the case not only for the diary but for his letters, photos, and everything that brought him close to Anna.

He struggled with the pen in his hand and tried to make it work against the paper.

Dear Anna,

Well, sweetheart, only two weeks left of tank training. We started firing our own rifles today. Our outfit had to march around with broom sticks all this time, the army was so short of rifles. The infantry had 'em all and I guess, since we are assigned to tanks, they figured we didn't need them that much.

I surprised myself and got the highest score in the platoon today. "Lucky" Joey Cipriano got the lowest. He says that's because they didn't let him have a machine gun—the kind he's used to, the kind all his family members in Jersey carry.

I laughed so hard I dropped my rifle. The sergeant on the firing line made me do one hundred push-ups and kiss my rifle, asking for forgiveness each time I went down. I had to say, "I'm sorry, baby, I won't do it again," every time I kissed it. He thought I was making fun of the rifle range and started yelling at me, "It ain't gonna be so damn funny when them Japs and Nazis start shooting back!" Sergeants have a way of saying things. I wonder if they're this tough under fire.

I've been doing plenty of push-ups lately. It seems like all we do is run, do push-ups, drill, then learn how to drive and take apart Sherman tanks. Now I wish I'd traded lines back in Boston with some guy who wanted out of the Army Air Corps.

They say we will be shipping out soon after training. Nobody knows where since we aren't engaged against the Germans yet. Most say that we'll go to England and wait for an invasion or something. Some of the guys in the class ahead of us are already gone. They won't tell us where, but the scuttlebutt says it's Ireland. I don't know why Ireland, but that's the family homeland. I'll be happy to spend the war there.

I can hear Uncle Billie excitedly saying, " 'Bout time America invaded somebody. May as well be them lads of the Emerald Isle." Give him my love, will ya? And that I am sorry I haven't written. I will write him this week.

I live for your letters. I keep them all safe inside the pillowcase. The guys would give me a heck of time if I actually used it for a pillow.

I'm taking it easy right now while the other guys in my outfit are out on the town. I just can't do it. All I think of is you and home. They all spend their money and end up broke. I'm stashing every penny away to give to you to save for our kid someday.

I don't know what to say. I have the pillowcase in one hand while I write this with the other. I'm afraid of wearing it out, but I love laying back on my bunk and dreaming of you. It smells like love to me when I do. Write soon. I love you darling.

Forever your husband,
Peter

He wished he could write better about his feelings. Anna could. She seemed almost poetic about it. She made putting words together seem easy, simple. So smart, she'd make sure all their children knew how to study, and each one would become somebody important someday.

One of the guys had a radio on. It played Benny Goodman. He laid back, put his head on the pillowcase propped up by his hands, and he listened with eyes closed, leaving the barracks behind for Port Hope Island and Anna.

19

PETER, I was getting worried," Anna said as they walked up the path leading to the cozy summer cottage she had rented for the weekend. "I wasn't sure you were coming today."

"Me, too," he smiled. "V-Mail was the best I could do. I thought about sending a telegram, but I didn't want to scare you . . . you know, nowadays with the War Department using them when a guy . . . well, you know."

"You're more handsome in uniform than I could have ever imagined," she blushed.

"Hey, if the uniform helps, I'll wear it after the war."

She looked up at him and smiled as they strolled arm in arm toward the beach house.

"How did you find this place?" he asked.

"A friend of the family owns it. I asked if it was vacant and explained about your two-day furlough, and before I could offer them any money, they told me where to find the keys. They said it was their wedding gift to us."

"Nice friends. I like 'em," he winked.

"Here we go," Anna said as she fumbled with the keys.

"Here, let me try, sweetheart," Peter said, reaching over for them. He unlocked the door. "This is really swell. It's like a dream," he said, turning to her and lifting her off her feet as they crossed into the small bungalow's living room.

"I love you so much, Peter."

They kissed, holding each other as if it were the first time, gently, tenderly.

"Maybe this is just a dream," he whispered in her ear.

"I have just the place to enjoy it," she invited, taking him by the hand.

He smiled, followed her, and kicked the bedroom door shut behind them.

The inlet was a private waterway with vacation cottages dotting the shoreline. On Connecticut's rugged southern shore, it was a few hours train ride from New York's Grand Central Station. They couldn't spend the time it took to get back to Port Hope Island, although Peter longed to see Uncle Billie and be home one more time before being sent into combat.

"Radioman is also the assistant tank driver and machine gunner," Peter finally admitted at Anna's urging as they walked barefoot along the white sandy shore. The silence that came back through the hurt look in her eyes, the worry and the tears, chilled him. He hadn't wanted her to believe his duty was dangerous. "I'll be alright. I promise. Joey is a madman in that tank. He was the highest-scoring driver in the unit. He's used to the crazy city drivers in Jersey. He used to drive a cab. Joey can handle outrunning a few Germans if anyone can. And you're looking at the best shot in the outfit," Peter said, seeking to appease her fears.

She looked up at him. Her eyebrows creased with sadness. Tears came easily but no words. She stopped, sat herself on the sandy beach and buried her head in her arms.

Peter sat, with arms around her, waiting, knowing he couldn't make make her any more promises other than he would be careful. He already had done that.

He watched the seagulls swooping down to the sand, circling on the breeze above, and thought how free they were. But then, maybe they didn't see it that way. He wondered if they worried, had concerns, or just lived to fly, eat, be part of the chain of events that made the ocean what it was.

The ocean was constant. Her waters ebbed back and forth along the shore. They gave life and took it away. He would be on them in hours, drifting towards war and only God knew what.

If he could fly above Anna, circle her with love, take the cares away, feed and clothe her and their soon-to-be child; if he could do that, be sure of it, he wouldn't ask for anything more.

"Anna, we have to be going. Only a few hours left."

"I want to go home with you to Port Hope," she cried softly. "I don't see you coming home, Peter. In my mind, I can't see you coming home to me." She covered her heaving body under his protective, muscular arms, and he was speechless.

He couldn't see himself coming home either. It was too distant, too unknown. No one knew how long the war would last, and all his optimism couldn't relieve the pangs of doubt.

He had been told the odds. The noncommissioned officers had told them that the average life expectancy of a tank crew in heavy fighting was four weeks, four months in sporadic fighting.

"Come on, darling," he finally urged, standing so that she would follow him along the beach to the cottage.

They walked silently through the surf, letting the foamy waves push the sea water across their feet, up their ankles, then knee deep. "Remember the first time we kissed?" Peter asked, stopping Anna as the water receded from their feet. "Remember?"

"Yes," she replied looking up into his questioning gaze.

"I was sixteen; you were fifteen. I was so in love with you then."

"I thought you would never try to kiss me." Anna brightened. "I turned my head, and you missed," she chuckled.

"I got better with practice," Peter teased, holding her slender waist. "Like this."

The *Queen Elizabeth* pulled out from the berthing. Peter thought he could see Anna waving on the dock. Every woman looked like Anna to him now. Her face, smile, eagerness to please him, make him feel wanted. . . . That was what he would remember. He decided that is what he would fight for.

Tug boats followed the converted luxury liner up the channel and past the Statue of Liberty. Army bands had bid the soldiers a farewell, and now the strains of silent tunes, still ringing in Peter's ears, mocked the sounds of white foamy streams of sea water splashing against the hull of the ship as it set out for open sea. It would make a rendezvous with Navy convoys headed for Great Britain. The soldiers were told to report on deck at 0600 hours the following morning for emergency drills, just in case a German U-boat was able to get through the ring of Navy steel surrounding the massive ocean liner, now a troop ship.

"Hey, Pete." A Jersey accent interrupted his thought.

"How's it goin', Joey," he returned, with eyes set to the dim outline of a distant shoreline and buildings.

"Not bad. Not bad. Say I hate to interrupt your thinkin', but some of the guys and me got some bets going. Why don't you come up to the top deck and join in? At least be there with me."

"Sure," Peter replied. "I've got nothing to lose. Nothing at all."

"It'll be good for ya to take your mind off things . . . ya know."

Joey pulled his Army tank companion under his arm and laid out the plan as they headed up ladders to the diversion Peter wanted so much now.

Anna made her way quietly through the milling crowd to the subway station and boarded for Grand Central. She wondered how long it would take to get a letter, how she would occupy her time between now and then.

Home to her parents' house in Hartford. At least she had hope. Her monthly female period had passed; she put her hand to her lower abdomen. She had part of him with her. Smiling, she exited the subway, made her way to the train station and home, to wait.

Uncle Billie walked his sheepdog, Laddie, down the steps to the beach. His energy wasn't what it used to be. He felt winded just going down, and now he looked back up and wondered how long it would take him to climb to the lighthouse. But he wanted to touch the water's edge, feel the tingle of coldness and wet sand squeeze between his toes, like a boy again.

"There we go, Laddie," he said, releasing the dog from a

leash to run along the sand. "I miss ya, boy," he sighed looking out at the pier.

How many days had he spent there, fishing pole in hand, feet draped over the edge, teaching Peter about the sea—about life? He had done his best, he knew. But the boy was grown up and gone too fast. Now this damnable war. He'd had his taste of it in the first one.

Not that long ago it seemed, but forever since he had touched the lips, caressed the soft skin of the only love in his life, Katie. She, too, had said her good-byes to him as he shipped out for a war. He knew how his boy, Peter, must be feeling now.

He strolled through the lapping waves, letting them kiss his feet with coldness. It was good. It wakened a tired man's blood. The ocean and William Robert O'Banyon had a long love and brief hate affair.

He stretched his limbs to step up to the pier and walk out to its edge with Laddie eagerly begging him to play, as they had so often in years before. "We're both too old for it now, Laddie. Or can't ya see it?" He smiled down at his canine companion who seemed to whimper an acknowledgment to him. "Aye . . . it hurts to know it, doesn't it, boy?" He looked out to the blue line marking the horizon, and his mind drifted plaintively back. It had to go back. That was where his life was . . . where his love was.

"That was over twenty years ago, right, Laddie?" Billie stroked the soft mane of his faithful Laddie as he gazed out to sea from the pier below the lighthouse. "Ah, Laddie, somehow I keep dreamin' that she will come back to me from her watery grave and hold me in her tender lovin' arms. If I keep the light on for her and jus' stay true to her, I . . . but it's jus' a dream . . . a grand dream, nothin' more."

"You're a good companion, ya know that, don't ya?" He patted his dog who whimpered a response, so eager to please his master. "That's what I like about ya, Laddie. No back talk. Come on. We must be lightin' the lamp now."

They reached the top of the stairs that led from the beach to the hill above. Billie stopped to catch his breath and look back out over the ocean he loved so well. "Ya miss Peter now, don't ya, Laddie? I miss him, too. Once this war is over, we'll be together again. We got 'ta keep this light bright for him, don't we, boy?"

The lighthouse keeper and his companion entered the door of the cottage attached to the front of the towering sentinel of Port Hope Island. "We best go fill the logbook and light the lamp now. A few words for the day, right, Laddie? Come on. One more set of stairs ta climb."

20

"ANNA, SWEETHEART?"

"Yes, Mom?"

"You'd better come to the door," her mother, Alice, said somberly.

Anna placed the last dish in the cupboard, took off her apron, and approached the door inquisitively.

"You Anna O'Banyon?" the young letter carrier asked.

She nodded anxiously while twisting her hands as her mother put her arms around her shoulders.

"This is for you, then. Good day, ladies," he tipped his hat and backed away from the porch.

"Mom! It can't be . . . not yet. He just . . ." She looked down at the yellow envelope in disbelief. She shakily fought to open the Western Union telegram.

Her mother held her breath as they both anxiously moved to the sofa in the living room of the comfortable Hartford, Connecticut home.

"Ah! Ha! Oh, Mom! Look!" she smiled. "When he gets

home, I'll knock his block off for scaring me like this," she
joyfully said, handing the telegram to her mother. She read:

MESSAGE: *Dear Anna . . . stop . . . I'm okay . . . stop . . .
Can't say where . . . stop . . . It'll be awhile before I can say
. . . stop . . . Tell Uncle Billie . . . stop . . . I love you all . . .
end.*

Anna hadn't heard from Peter for almost one month. Except
for bombing raids, the newspapers were silent on the war in
Europe involving U.S. troops. She knew he had been in Ireland; that was all.

"I've got to let Uncle Billie know. Where's that telephone
number for the Port Hope Island Ferry office?" Anna asked
her mother excitedly.

"Strange. The light is still on from last night. Hello, Billie?"
Hal, the middle-aged postman and all-purpose office manager
at the ferry office called out as he pulled his sidecar motorcycle
up to the door of the lighthouse. "Hello! Anybody here?" He
peered through the window.

"Billie!" Hal called out, rapping on the window. "Billie?"
Billie's sheepdog came to the bay window and whimpered,
paws propped against the glass windowpane.

Hal anxiously grabbed at the front-door handle. The door
flew open against his weight. There in front of him lay Billie
with Laddie, his dog, nuzzled up against his body.

"Billie. Billie? You hear me, Billie?" Hal asked gently as he
leaned over and nudged the lighthouse keeper.

Billie opened his eyes slowly. His hands reached for his chest
as he attempted to speak. "Climbing stairs. Chest . . . Hal get
me doctor," he weakly voiced.

"Come on, old buddy. Can you sit up? I'll get ya to your car, and we'll take you over by ferry to Nantucket to see Dr. O'Neal."

Hal put Billie's arm around his neck, lifted him to his feet, and then hefted the large man into his muscular arms. "Good thing I stay in shape," he smiled to Billie. "Your buddy, Hal, will take care of you. Come on, Laddie," he called to the dog.

"Uncle Billie?" Anna called softly. "I'm here. It's Anna," she said as she leaned over his hospital bed and gave him a kiss on the cheek.

"Oh, Anna, darlin'," he mouthed feebly. "You're like an angel," his eyes brightened. "I thought I noticed more light in this room," he smiled.

"You are a charmer," she laughed, pulling a chair up next to the bed.

"I thought maybe I was a goner," Billie voiced. "It was your call to Hal at the ferry that saved me. He came to tell me you called and found me flat on my back. Not a very dignified position for a lighthouse keeper," he grinned.

"I called to tell you I heard from Peter," she smiled, stroking his hand. "He sent a telegram telling us he's okay but couldn't say where he is. I guess they shipped the First Armored Division to Ireland, but no one knows where they'll go next."

"North Africa," Billie whispered with strained breath.

"How do you know?" Anna asked surprised.

"A lightkeeper's hunch. Besides, that's where the tank battles are between the Germans and the English. It will be North Africa." The effort to speak had put considerable strain on the aged man of the sea.

Anna patted his hand. "You get some sleep now. I'll be right here when you wake up."

21

HOW IMMEASURABLY *short life really is,* the eighteen-year-old bride thought. Why had it never occurred to her before? Because she was young. *Life goes on to fifty, sixty, seventy, eighty years, doesn't it?* She had never been concerned because the end was so many decades ahead.

Now, the hometown newspapers listed the increasing number of war dead. Eighteen years old, nineteen, twenty . . . these people she knew. Peter was nineteen years old.

She picked up the latest letter from Peter. *He is alive, isn't he?* She knew two people from home in Hartford who had boy friends in the service, both on Guadalcanal. Both friends received letters the same week only to discover their boy friends, Marines, had been killed in action two weeks before the letters actually arrived. *Peter surely is alive,* she reassured herself.

She wanted to be here, at the lighthouse, close as she could be to Peter and a home the way she dreamed of. She felt good about taking care of bedridden Uncle Billie and wasn't sure she should let Peter know. Billie had asked her not to write nor to worry Peter about his health. He didn't want Peter preoccupied during the upcoming battle.

She had tearfully asked Uncle Billie for reassurance. "Peter will come back, won't he?"

"Aye, lass. The small voice inside me reassures it. He's the last of the O'Banyons. I've got a feelin', though I cannot tell ye for sure, but just a feelin' his Da will watch over him. It's something I just feel. Don't ye worry. He'll be back."

She looked down to the letter she had already read a dozen times.

October 1942

My Darling Anna,

We are aboard ship. I cannot say where for sure. Now that we left Ireland I guess I can say that is where I have been these past months. The censors may cut out words here or there, but I will write them anyway.

I got letters from you every week while we were there. A lot of the guys are jealous because of that. Some of these poor fellas have gotten just one letter in a month. Two friends of mine got "Dear Johns." Both of their girls went for Navy men instead. You should see 'em aboard ship. They're ready to go at it with the first sailor that looks cross-eyed at them.

I knocked all of my platoon buddies out when I showed them the picture of you in the bathing suit on the beach. This one guy who has a thing for red heads offered me money. Says he knows how to get the photo enlarged, and he wanted a real pin-up girl, not one of those Hollywood dames. He said he would trade me his first weekend pass. How about that? He knew I wouldn't give it up. But it sure made me proud to have guys say, "Man, will you get a load of this," when I passed your picture around.

I've been writing just a few words a day in that War Diary. I'm not so good with words. I sit down to write, and my thoughts won't come out in ink. It's frustrating. So I just put down what happens. Not very dramatic I'm afraid. Maybe once we are in battle.

Battle doesn't seem like a real thing to me. We're out here on this troop ship in the Atlantic somewhere, zigzagging around because the brass is afraid of submarines. I guess they can't hit the ship if it's zigzagging. A lot of the guys get sick from the pitch of the ship in rough seas. I kind of like it. I lay back, put a smile on my face, and dream about being on the lighthouse skiff, or sailing like we used to with Hal's sixteen-footer down at the dock.

We must have sailed over a hundred times together. I wish I was doing that now. Just sailing, drifting along Port Hope, shooting over to Nantucket during the Fourth of July race. It always leads to the beach, the blanket, just you and me at moonlight. Man, what I wouldn't give for that now.

It's almost mail call. I'll send this with all my love. We are headed for the fight, sweetheart. I know you pray for me. Pray for my tank crew, too, will ya? Joey, he's in trouble most of the time, gambling or drinking, but he's okay. Then there's the gunner, Mike Meyers from St. Paul, Minnesota. He's our scholar, always reading a book, and our tank commander Sergeant Doug Clamser, I think from L.A. or near there. He's a real swell guy. You'd like him. He's always talking about home, his wife, and two kids. He's the old man. Twenty-six, I think.

Well, got to go. I think about you always. I love you, darling.

> *Your husband,*
> *Peter*

Anna moved slowly across the room to the window. Uncle Billie lay still, breathing easy. The sound of aircraft engines brought her outside. An entire formation of flying fortresses headed east, to England, she supposed. And out on that ocean was her beloved with thousands of other men heading into a violent unknown.

She rubbed her arms from sudden chills sweeping over her. The breeze was gentle, though. The aircraft were disappearing now, swallowed into the white, billowing sculptures floating effortlessly against the azure heights of space. Life seemed so unfair.

The joy of nothing more than holding hands and kicking sand along the beach was too easily destroyed by the eagerness of madmen killing the troops of other madmen. Oh, Roosevelt wasn't a madman, but she wondered what it would be like if the men doing all the fighting just said no. That damnable Hitler and Tojo ought to be shot. Then they'd finally get it . . . the glory there is in killing. It made her mad. *Doesn't anyone in Germany or Japan have the courage to get rid of them?*

Anna returned to her duty. She was caring for Uncle Billie until he could handle the light again. She loved it in the lighthouse. Except for Peter being gone from it, it was the only place on earth she'd rather be. And Uncle Billie was an adorable old *gentleman*. So few men could hold a candle to him; she wondered if he knew it.

Watching him sleep peacefully with his sheepdog, Laddie, by his side, she wondered what it was that had brought him here in the first place. Peter had never made it clear, and she hadn't asked him to tell her about his past. Not yet, anyway. Sure Billie had told her the name of the woman he had married and adored, Katie. But that was all.

Who really is the mystery lady in the photograph? Anna walked over to the mantle and picked up the silver-framed black and white photograph where an aged-brass ship's clock sat. "From the grateful crew of the *Othello,*" said the inscription.

The photo revealed a happy couple at Coney Island with their little one some summer lost in time long ago.

She was pretty, and the man with her in the photograph holding the baby was as handsome as Peter: square-jawed, broad-shouldered, not too tall, but neither short, just firmly lithe and strong; deep, penetrating eyes of serious blue and wisps of blond running through a full head of auburn hair brushed neatly to the side.

The young woman was an elegant and gracious woman of blessed countenance. *Beautiful* was a word invented for her. She looked to possibly be a red head—like her, she imagined—fair-skinned. It could be she and Peter standing there, if dressed in 1920-era clothes. What happened to her? Was she the reason Billie kept the light to sea?

Next, she walked past the potbelly stove to the neat but small roll-top desk. There sat the lighthouse logbook. *What would the pages reveal?* She wondered if there was more she could learn about her own beloved husband by finding out about this man, Billie O'Banyon, almost brought to the end of his life by heart attack. She picked up the heavy leather-bound volume and walked to the sofa facing the bay window overlooking the sea and began to read.

The Lighthouse Keeper

June 28, 1919

I arrived today from the mainland to start my service as lighthouse keeper at the new station on a small isle off greater Nantucket Island called Port Hope. The story is told about a light appearing in the night to save a 1600's pilgrim ship from certain destruction. Come daybreak, they saw this isle, landed, prayed their thanks, and so named it as it now stands.

At first sight, the lighthouse was grand and glorious to behold, the towering white structure capped with a glass surrounded turret. I felt like the captain of a ship as I stopped atop her and gazed out to sea. "Lead Kindly Light," the Christian hymn, suddenly came to me in the silence. I swear it did. Where it came from I cannot tell, but it was as if the angels themselves were playin' with my mind. I'm not given much to hymns, especially since last year when I felt God had abandoned me. But my darlin' Kathleen sang hymns, though I never paid much mind to them.

I've been angry at losin' my Katie and our boy, Alexander. Although I felt coming here was right, I couldn't resolve myself to this fate of solitary confinement in a paradise such as this without them. Why, God? I've asked myself over and over again.

Ah, Katie would love it here. I still hear her words to me when we first walked the beach on our honeymoon at Nantucket Bay so long ago. "Would ye not think it grand, William, ta raise our wee ones far from the teeming city, here along the ocean's pleasant shore?"

"Aye, that I would. It would be grand, mighty pleasin'," I said as I held her in my arms. Ah, dear God in heaven, this is a lighthouse logbook, not some journal of a lonely, lost soul.

But I seem to hear her voice come to me today, here on the island. I walked from the lighthouse door, flowers of every kind brushing against my legs, cushioning my walk, and strangely felt I was on holy ground. I couldn't walk around the budding carpet of rainbow colors and field grass so green. I had to walk through.

The thought occurred as I did that no one walks around life. No one. Only through, whatever that may bring. Where do these comfortin' thoughts come from? I cannot tell. Do they erase the pangs of pain and doubt? Make it all okay? No. I hurt still.

But as I crushed the many-colored flower pedals beneath my feet makin' my way to the edge of the hill upon which stands the towerin' lighthouse, it was as if the plant life were saying, "We live to please you."

I took my path to the point where a rolling hill of sand and coastal herbage slopes gently down to the beach. A small pier is there. I imagined my lady standing on it, beckoning me to come, relax, hold hands—be by her side.

Our ship sailed near here to Ireland last year, and I came back along this shore without her and my laddie.

I'll be puttin' the light out for her. Maybe she will come. Maybe she'll walk right back from the sea. Whatever ship may profit from the lighthouse, I will be glad, but I'll just be doing my job. Fer what? Money? Hah, the fool I was all those years worryin' about it.

No, the light is for Katie and my lad, forever for them. I will try to sleep this first night prayerfully thanking God to be watchin' if this tune in my head will leave me to slumber.

I still feel like askin', "Dear God, why?" Somehow in my mind I hear Father Shannon's words, "He'll lift ye up, lad. Surely he will."

Anna wiped at the moisture welling in her eyes. What a dear, sweet man she loved, and now she knew why he was the way he was.

She had the lighthouse keeper, Billie, to thank for that. She began to hum without thinking about it. An old-time melody she had heard for as many Sundays as she had gone to church with her parents. She found herself humming it with eyes closed. It was John Henry Newman's hundred-year-old melody.

Lead kindly Light, amid the encircling gloom;
Lead thou me on!
The night is dark, and I am far from home;
Lead thou me on!
Keep thou my feet; I do not ask to see,
The distant scene—One step enough for me!

So long thy power hath blessed me, sure it still
Will lead me on.
O'er moor and fen, o'er crag and torrent, till
*   The night is gone.*
And with the morn those angel faces smile,
Which I have loved long since, and lost awhile!

22

PETER AND Joey Cipriano arrived in Northern Ireland in October 1942 with their tank outfit to a camp just outside of Belfast where other regiments of the First Armored Division had already been in training for some months. By the fall of 1942, the United States had been engaged against the Japanese in the Pacific but had not yet entered the fight against Hitler's forces in Europe or Africa.

To Peter, this was the greatest thing the Army had done for him. His mother and father and all his relatives were from southern Ireland, and here he was, all expenses paid, standing on sacred Irish soil. Peter admired the beautiful land but could tell it was a hard land, too. The land required that you love it with hard, back-breaking work or leave it for the American dream. He understood much more about his Uncle Billie now that he could breathe Irish air and gaze upon her rolling land of small farms and quaint villages.

Although the soldiers could write home, their letters were heavily censored by the Army. They weren't allowed to say exactly where they were stationed for fear of tipping off German intelligence. But Peter could add his own little code so he mentioned to Anna that he kissed the "Blarney Stone" while on leave and to tell Uncle Billie a "leprechaun" in Army green sent him love from the other end of the rainbow.

Most of the men with Peter were draftees. There were very few regular Army men in the outfit in those days. To a man, they were eager to get on with the war and go home. They trained each day in the green pastoral terrain competing against other battalions in mock tank attacks. Joey was at the controls, Peter manned the radio and turret machine guns, and Sergeant Bill Clamser, from Los Angeles, commanded the Sherman tank.

To a certain point, Peter and Joey found "playing Army" was fun. No one got hurt. They were young, confident, and anxious to go against the Germans and prove themselves. At that time, there was a typical American self-assurance about winning the war in a decisive and quick way simply because the US Army were "the good guys," the cavalry to the rescue.

The Army made sure that all the *fun* the tank units had driving the Shermans through the Irish countryside was punctuated with a good dose of boredom. Everyone pulled guard duty at least one or two nights per week.

One particularly miserable cold and wet night, a soldier pulling guard duty in Peter's platoon got sick. It meant one of the others, who had passes to go out on the town, would have to take his place.

Peter had no particular desire to go out to a pub somewhere and watch everyone else get smashed, since he wasn't a real drinker. He knew Joey wouldn't give up his pass; boozing and gambling were in his blood; he was in a constant state of readiness to party.

Joey had this thing about Peter being good luck for him. Peter would leave a crap game; Joey would begin to lose. He would return, and Joey would win. It got so that Joey wouldn't play unless his pal Pete was there.

This night was different. There was a boxing match in town, and Joey had his man all figured out.

"You gotta go with me, Pete," he demanded. "All ya got to do is stand there and watch. I'll even front ya some dough if that's the problem. When you see the paws on this guy I'm bettin' on, you'll want to wager, too."

"Someone has got to cover for Evans. You go. This isn't cards or craps. Just don't bet everything on your man," Peter replied.

"Hey, Pete. Come on. Evans isn't even in our squad. You're ruining a perfectly beautiful night. I've got this Irish dame I met at the PX the other day meeting us there. Afterwards . . . who knows? You've got to loosen up," Joey urged with a slap on Peter's shoulder.

Peter grabbed his helmet, web belt with side arm, ammo clips, M1 rifle, and headed for the door. "I got to go now, Joey. Don't stick your neck out too far."

"One of these days you're going to be sorry you left me out there on my own. It will be your hind end in a sling wondering where lucky Joey is. You'll see. Aw . . . go on," he waved and left the opposite end of the Quonset hut barracks.

Peter was ordered to guard duty at the commanding officer's hut. The rain was coming down in torrents as he sloshed along back and forth at a boring hundred paces until the next sentry was encountered.

Though they wore ponchos over their uniforms, somehow the rain got through until both sentries were entirely soaked.

"I'd give anything to get out of this rain. Man, it never stops," complained the other sentry.

Peter sneezed. "You got to be Irish to love it," Peter called back. It was about midnight, and he was due to be relieved. Suddenly, a Willeys appeared out of the wet blackness with two MP's and an obviously unconscious soldier seated between them. The soldier's head bobbed around with each rut they encountered in the muddy road.

"Halt! Who goes there?" Peter said loudly.

"Military police, soldier," the driver answered.

"How'd we end up at the CO's hut? What's wrong with you, Corporal," asked one of the MP's holding the drunk soldier up in the back seat.

"You're the smart one with all the answers. I say we go left, you say right. Hell, in all this rain, pitch black out there, water over the wheel wells, you expect me maybe to use radar?"

"Ah, shut your lousy trap! You're supposed to know the turnoff to the stockade," the MP wearing sergeant stripes in the back of the jeep growled.

"Hey, buddy. We missed the turnoff to the stockade. Damn, won't this rain ever quit?" the jeep's driver groaned as he tried to speak through the noise of the pelting rain and jeep's engine. "Which way to the stockade?"

"Why don't I take this man off your hands?" Peter offered. Dead-drunk Joey sat there moaning pitifully. Peter knew if he went to the stockade and was busted or sent to court martial, he stood to have another driver assigned to their tank for the duration of the war. Joey had his problems, but the two opposites had become like brothers.

"I said I'll take him. Look, here's my replacement now," Peter pointed to another soldier coming out of the CO's hut.

"Look, I know this man. I'll take him in to the CO and write up a report on him. Why don't you guys get out of the rain?"

"Hey, come on, Sarge," the driver pleaded. "If this guard says he knows him, what's it gonna hurt letting him sleep it off in his own bunk? Let him take this drunk with him. We could be out here all night looking for the turnoff to the stockade. He's not worth dying from pneumonia over."

The husky MP in the back yanked on Joey's arm which was attached to his wrist by handcuff. "I'll be glad to get rid of this loser," the sergeant snapped back as he took his key and released Joey. "I expect to be back in the morning to get this guy. Have him ready at 0800 hours."

"Sure thing, Sergeant," Peter called back over the noise. "Here, let me have him," Peter said as the MP leaned Joey up against him.

"0800 hours," the sergeant called as the jeep took off.

"Joey. Joey. It's me, you lucky son of a gun. Hey, what did you go and do now?" Peter asked as he dragged him up the steps and into the warmth of the hut's entry. "Here, sit down. There we go. You're a lot of trouble sometimes, you know that?"

Joey's eye's opened slowly as he focused up towards Peter. "Hey, ol' buddy. How'd you get here?" he slurred as his chin dropped back down to his chest.

The desk sergeant on duty came over with a cup of coffee.

"Thanks," Peter offered as he tried lifting Joey's chin up to get him to take a sip.

"Hey. That's for you, not for him. You're going to need all the strength you got to lug that character back to the barracks."

"Oh, yeah. Thanks." Peter sniffled. He was physically spent from six hours in the rain. Draining the cup, he hunched over and hefted Joey onto his shoulders. "Come on. It's time for Pete to take you home."

Joey slapped at him with a pat on the head. "You're so good to me. You, my Pete! Lucky Pete!" he slobbered.

"Joey! Joey! Come on, man. They just blew reveille. We're shipping out. Come on, we got to get our gear together," Peter urged him the next morning.

"Oh, man, leave me alone. I wanna die. Just leave me!" he moaned, waving Peter off.

"Joey, I can't leave you. We're headed out. Now. Today. This is it, man. We're headed for action. Come on, get up," he prodded as he swung him out of bed and let him hit hard on the floor.

"Hey, what ya do that for?" he groused.

"You idiot. Can't you remember a thing? I pulled your rear end out of the fire again last night. Remember?"

"All I remember is my man lost. I lost everything, see. If you'd been there, I would've won," he slowly grumbled. "Then I went to a bar. There was this fight over this dame, what's her name . . . and I took a bottle of whiskey. That's all. I don't feel so good."

"Man, you'd think I was your big brother always looking out for you like I do. When we get into action, you owe me some good driving. Get dressed. I'll help pack your gear."

Joey looked up to Peter with as serious a look as a man with a hangover can. "Don't ever leave me out there, Pete," he said earnestly. "I mean it. I trust you. You bring me luck. You stick by me out there, when we fight, okay? Something happens and you bring me back."

He was a sad-looking nut case, but Peter liked him. "Yeah, sure. I'm your good-luck charm, right?"

NOVEMBER 8, 1942
ORAN, ALGIERS
FRENCH NORTH AFRICA

"Get that damn Vichy sniper," Sergeant Clamser barked. Joey wheeled the lumbering tank to the right and then to the left as a squad of armored infantry followed close behind them.

They had met light resistance from the French Vichy allies of the German Reich on their initial landings on beaches north of Oran.

The Germans themselves were being driven west by the English from the fighting going on in Libya. The inexperienced Americans had landed west of the fighting to convince the French to join them against the real enemy, the Germans, then attack east to trap the Germans between them and the English. But there were French diehards, saboteurs, snipers, and a garrison near the Tafaraoui airfield that had determined to defend their honor.

Peter found himself at the radio with hands on the tank's .30-caliber machine guns, looking through the slits widely for any sign of movement in the buildings ahead. The infantry opened up at a man elevated on the roof tops as he arched back to throw a grenade.

"There, three o'clock, on the roof," the sergeant yelled as he opened with the turret gun on the lone man. Peter watched as the man fell from the building, grenade flying free and rolling toward them. Explosion, smoke, debris. Silence.

"Scratch one Vichy," shouted the tank commander from the turret gun.

Peter stared at the dead man through the gunsight slits from inside the tank. Joey backed the tank up as the infantry dragged the corpse from the street. Other light and medium

M3 Grants and Shermans from the First Armored Division were headed from east and west toward the main downtown intersection. Oran had been secured on their first day of battle without a loss to the new men from Combat Command B.

There was little time for reflection on the killing of the Frenchman as the tanks formed a column and were now ordered west to help take the airfield.

"He was a brave man, don't ya think, Joey?"

"Who?"

"The French sniper," Peter replied.

"More like stupid or suicidal if ya ask me."

"Stupid," answered Clamser.

"Yeah. Stupid and suicidal," Joey offered back. "What's a Frenchman fighting for the Germans, anyway?"

"These guys, the Vichy French, believe that Germany's got the muscle, and they wanted to be on the winning side. This French Marshall Pétain, their leader . . . he's a real traitor if you ask me," Peter responded.

"What's a 'Vichy' anyway?" Joey asked.

"It's a place in France where Pétain runs a goose-stepping Nazi French Government. They won't last long if they keep fighting like this," Sergeant Clamser responded. "We got firing up ahead. You get those directions over the radio, O'Banyon?"

"Left one-quarter mile, airdrome tower should be off the right flank. Fire upon Lt. Cummings orders, on smoke," Peter repeated.

"Roger that. Left one-quarter mile coming up," Joey smiled at the controls. "Kinda fun, huh Pete?"

"Kinda fun? Sailing a boat off Port Hope is kinda fun. You're nuts, Joey."

"Crazy like a back-alley slot machine," he grinned. "I can't wait till these stupid Frenchies give up so I can teach them how to shoot dice instead of Americans. If they're this stupid now, they'll be double stupid when I get through with them. Look out, chickadees. We's headed for the Casbah." Joey laughed. Peter grinned.

DECEMBER 10, 1942
PORT HOPE ISLAND

Anna helped Uncle Billie with the wash, mended some socks, and was finishing the dishes as he started to settle back into being home.

"I light the lamp tonight, okay, Uncle Billie?"

"Are you sure ya can handle the stairs, darlin?"

"What? Of course. Don't you worry. This baby still has three months to go, and she's never been a problem yet," she said patting her swollen stomach.

"*He* hasn't been, ya mean?" Billie grinned.

"She," Anna smiled.

"Ya remember how the wick works and the oil level and that lighter match; how ya wait till the latch is secure on the pot before lighten' the wick?"

"Yes, Uncle Billie," she returned with raised eyebrow. "Now you make sure Hal remembers when he comes up each night to help you when I leave to have this baby."

"Aye, that I will," he chuckled. "Aw, Katie would've loved this place. How I'd love to hold her hand once more, watch the light shine out to sea with her. How very grand it might have been."

There was a moment of silence as Anna visualized Billie as a young man, eyes glistening with the joy of another time, but now trapped in an older man's body.

"I'll have the light on for you, Uncle Billie, and be right down," she said softly.

He cast his gaze to sea. The mighty Atlantic had taught him so much in so short of time: her currents, waves, life, and abundance. Katie was a part of her, too. Mankind owed the sea its very life, if it came right down to it. Billie couldn't blame the sea for taking his love so many years ago. He simply must be part of her and not regret. He'd never have become a lightkeeper had it not been for the call of the sea.

He looked up on the wall above the bronze ship's clock, the one from the main bridge on the *Othello*, a gift from the crew so many years ago. Above the clock was the remembrance that had finally brought him peace and led him to a grander purpose in life than mere day-to-day survival.

Father Shannon was right that day he had given it to him so many years ago. The wall decoration offered the secret. "He will lift ya up, laddie. He surely will if ya just believe with all yer heart," Father Shannon had said.

"A light shall break forth from the darkness. . . ." he said aloud as he patted his sheepdog who slept comfortably at his feet.

His voice echoed up the spiral stairs as Anna struck a match to the wick that set the mighty beam apart from all other lighthouses. This one, not automated by electricity like the rest, had survived the changes over the years to stand as a lonely sentinel where man and beam together worked to offer light to those in the forbidding darkness at sea.

That thought struck Anna in a way it never had before. Casting her eyes out to the bay, she could see the pier and could hear Peter's voice calling her, teasing her, loving her. Thoughts of him engaged in battle caused her to shudder.

Uncle Billie had taught her about a greater light than all the others. That light's power over darkness and despair comforted her now. For weeks he had reminisced and given her the full story on what had brought him here, and she owed him gratitude for the clarity it brought her.

Now she understood Peter, what made him so very different from other men she had met and known. "Here, on this island, there will always be a lightkeeper, Uncle Billie. I promise you," she whispered like a prayer as she descended to care for the man from Cork.

23

"COME ON, Myers, dammit! Sight that damn Kraut in, will ya?" Sergeant Clamser yelled from his perch in the turret as he fired the .50 caliber in defiance of the rapidly advancing German troops.

"He's dead, Sarge," Peter yelled as he beat his hand against the radio. "The radio is out. That hit we took . . ." Peter grimaced at the sight of Myers wedged between his seat and the 75-millimeter loading breach. Joey tried desperately to restart the engine.

"Out! Out! Out! Now!" Clamser shouted as he held off a patrol of enemy troops who now crouched in firing position behind their lead tank less than one hundred meters away. "Go, go, go!" he screamed, firing all the while. The German

Mark VI swung its huge 88 millimeter gun muzzle toward them.

Joey and Peter moved as quickly as they could, down the escape hatch on the deck of their Sherman that was now smoking from the enemy shell that had grazed their hull on the back side.

They scrambled from the tank to some nearby rocks, leaping as they ran over the corpses of American infantry who had been surprised by the sudden fury of the Nazi Panzer attack.

"We got to go back. . . . Clamser is holding those guys for us," Peter screamed above the deafening noise of cannon fire and artillery explosions.

Joey grabbed him as Peter started to dart from the safety of the massive boulders they crouched behind. "No, Pete. We do as Clamser ordered."

"We can't leave him there to die!" Peter protested. As he did, a sudden explosion rocked the tank onto its side, and it erupted into flames.

Peter stood entranced.

"Get down! Let's get the hell out of here!" Joey screamed above the violence of automatic gun fire and explosions. "Grab a rifle!" he yelled to Peter as he ran from the cover of the rocks to a dead American soldier and picked up his Thompson submachine gun. Joey ran beyond the soldier towards an ammunition truck sitting with a bullet-riddled driver slumped over at the wheel. The engine was still running.

I've got to save Clamser, Peter thought to himself. The flames roared from their burning tank. Reason had flown from him as suddenly as the fury of destruction had wiped out their entire lead platoon of tanks and infantry.

The fire, he thought to himself. Explosions rained desert

sand upon him as he began to run toward his sergeant who stumbled toward him, clothes ablaze.

Joey looked around for Peter, his good-luck charm. "Peter! You can't do anything for him! Dammit to hell," he raged. Pulling the dead driver from the truck seat, Joey put his foot to the floor and headed across the dry, dust-blown Tunisian battleground that had become a death trap for his comrades. Explosions rocked the truck, and he couldn't make out more than a few yards ahead of him.

A few straggling infantrymen broke from the cover of the rocky mounds of Kasserine Pass and tried to make it to the moving truck, but they were mowed down by fire from German troops just yards away.

I wouldn't do this for anyone else, Joey said to himself as he urgently gunned the six-cylinder duce-and-a-half supply truck directly toward Peter, who stooped down to a charred Sergeant Clamser, throwing him over his shoulder.

"Live, Clamser," Peter breathed desperately. "Live, damn you. Live!" he demanded as he ran with the wounded man toward the oncoming truck.

"Throw him in the back!" Joey shouted above the din as he swung around to meet Peter on a full dead run with artillery now zeroed in on them.

Peter jumped with his load upon the bumper and fell into the canvas-covered truck bed as Joey sped in full retreat toward the fleeing American columns.

"Hell, Peter! Don't ever make me do that again!" Joey yelled back as he maneuvered in and out of burning vehicles, blown-apart tanks, trying to avoid bodies of First Infantry Division soldiers littering the field for what seemed like forever.

Peter looked wide-eyed at Joey. Joey looked for a split second into the rearview mirror. "You are the luckiest SOB in the whole damn First Armored Division. You know that?" he growled. "Crazy . . ." he grumbled as they reached a point beyond the enemy artillery.

Peter glanced down at Clamser whose head rested in his lap. With pain-tortured expression, his sergeant's voice gurgled in an attempt to speak. Then his eyes rolled back as his hand reached suddenly to grab Peter's fatigues. He gritted his teeth in a desperate attempt. "Wife . . . Mary . . ." he struggled. "I . . . oh, no! God!" he began shivering uncontrollably.

"Don't die, Sarge," Peter pled. "You can make it," he urged as the truck sped across the desert in a race with a hundred other trucks, jeeps, and tanks in full retreat. Peter looked out the back of the truck. He could see the dust of a massive column of German armor a mile or so behind. He looked back to Clamser. The tank commander's grip relaxed, and he lay still, clothing smoking and partially burned away.

"Don't die!" Peter yelled above the noise as he held the man against his own body. "Don't die!"

24

THE RETREAT from Kasserine Pass was a well-organized affair that our boys pulled off with modest casualties. Our fellas inflicted heavy losses on the attacking Axis forces when . . ." the radio announcer's voice was drowned out by the guffaws and cat calls of the wounded.

"Oh, yeah, you jackass . . . I'm a modest casualty?" A chest-wounded soldier coughed sarcastically.

"Modest my . . ." another spit out with explicatives too numerous to count. "Who writes that horse s—" as his voice was deadened by an entire tent full of wounded and battle-hardened soldiers adding their counters to the army account of the complete and utter route the German's had given them.

"Pack of lies . . . My whole squad is dead. That SOB's never even been near the business end of a German gun," grumbled another bandaged soldier.

"The next song is dedicated to all you tank jockeys from the First Armored Division who so gallantly held off the attacking

Panzer units while our boys in the infantry regrouped for the upcoming counter offensive."

More hoots and hallooing.

"Now for more popular music, we bring you Fred Astaire and his new hit "Cheek to Cheek" with Irving Berlin and his orchestra. This has been another Armed Forces Radio News broadcast to all our men in North Africa. God speed and good luck:

The noise in the tent mellowed to the silver, crooning tones of Fred Astaire.

Heaven,
I'm in heaven,
And my heart beats so that I can hardly speak,
And I seem to find the happiness I seek,
When we're out together dancing cheek to cheek.

Heaven, I'm in heaven,
And the cares that hung around me through the week,

A soldier laughed loudly and harmonized with Astaire:

Seem to vanish like a gambler's lucky streak,

The tent full of sick and wounded now cheerily chimed in:

"When we we're out together dancing cheek to cheek."

They continued in a raspy, horse, offbeat, happy, out-of-tune chorus, some so weak they could barely move their lips. But they were alive and seemed to collectively and instinctively know, as one fell in after another, that to sing meant they couldn't die.

The tent of fifty beds rocked:

Oh, I love to climb a mountain,
And to reach the highest peak,
But it doesn't thrill me half as much,
As dancing cheek to cheek.

Oh, I love to go out fishing,
In a river or a creek,
But I don't enjoy it half as much,
As dancing cheek to cheek.

Two walking-wounded on crutches hammed it up in pantomine.

Dance with me,
I want my arm about you.
The charm about you,
Will carry me through!

Loud laughter and hand clapping seemed to sway the hospital tent as the wounded watched their two comrades swing with cheeks pressed up to each other.

To heaven;

They all joined as another soldier cheerfully waved a thermometer to the beat:

I'm in heaven,
And my heart beats so that I can hardly speak,
And I seem to find the happiness I seek,
When we're out together dancing cheek to cheek."

Music's magical medicine had potently charged new life into the bedraggled bunch of wounded men. A nurse tried in vain to quiet the raucous and spontaneous celebration for the benefit of the deathly sick and seriously wounded.

To the relief of the hospital ward, the asinine assertions of the army's radio jockey behind the lines in Casablanca, Morocco, mixed with the words summoning *heaven*—a place too many of their buddies knew at too young an age—had some men in tearful hysterics, a balm from endless days of fear and pain.

Peter walked over to the radio and turned it off.

"Hey, what the hell do you think you're doing?" an angry, shirtless, teenage soldier, propped on his pillow, yelled from across the makeshift desert-tent hospital room.

Peter ignored him.

"Hey, come on, Mac, turn it back on," called another wounded soldier.

The entire tent's wrath turned on Corporal Peter O'Banyon, it seemed. Epithets, threats, and cursing rolled off him like water off a duck's back as he stared down at Sergeant Clamser, bandaged from head to toe, barely breathing with the aid of an oxygen mask.

He watched in a state of complete silence and stillness, unaware of the room's noisy calls for the music to be turned back on. He was absorbed not only in the desperate struggle his tank commander was going through but also in thoughts of home.

This guy wants to get back and is hanging on for the wife and two kids, Peter thought. It was the only thing Peter could believe kept him alive.

Clamser had been totally in flames one minute, a shot-up hulk of burning flesh, then scooped into Peter's arms as he scrambled for their lives, begging for Clamser to live.

Clamser suddenly jerked, and his body arched as if he was being stabbed from underneath the thin hospital mattress.

"Doctor! Medic! Anyone!" Peter called out.

A nurse came quickly to the bedside, throwing back the mosquito tent that enveloped Clamser's body.

"More oxygen!" she pointed urgently to the bottle.

Peter began to turn it up, watching for the nurse's signal.

The doctor arrived, a captain. "Relax, Nurse Spencer. This one's gone," he said with a quick eye check and cursory breathing exam. "Ship him out to the morgue. We have more wounded coming in. We'll need this bed."

"Just like that?" Peter tiredly asked, standing in the way as the doctor tried to move to another patient's bed.

"Stand aside, soldier."

"No, sir. You help my buddy. You make him live."

"I said stand aside. Stand aside before I call the MP's."

"They any worse than German 88s? Tiger tanks maybe?"

"You are in real trouble if you don't let me pass."

Peter looked directly into the eyes of the calloused medical officer. He placed his right hand on his sidearm. "Check him out," he said firmly, manly. Peter O'Banyon, the boy, had died at Kasserine.

"Do you know what you're doing?" asked the stunned captain, backing away from Peter. "Corporal, if this is some sort of bad joke, we can settle this here and now by you taking your hand off that weapon."

Peter removed the Colt .45 pistol from his holster and yanked the slide back to a firing position. "You'll take another look, sir. He's got a wife and two kids. He saved my life. I've got to do the same. Look at him, please," Peter stated slowly and directly as he raised his handgun to the level of the officer's chest. Empty, dangerous eyes sighted the captain in.

The doctor turned nervously to the bed of the dead sergeant and motioned with his head for the nurse to depart, to summon help.

Peter, covered with the grime of battle, stared at the doctor in complete disregard for any conventions of military compliance or discipline.

The medical officer took in Peter's blank, uninterested, fatigued, and fearless expression, turned to face the deathly still tank commander.

He placed his stethoscope above the bandages at the center of Clamser's chest. Dropping the stethoscope, he felt for pulse.

"Nurse! Get me—" He rattled off something and added "Quickly!" to a nurse nearby, huddled in fear with two others.

"But . . ." the nurse began to protest.

"Now!" the captain ordered. "Get the adrenaline injection *now!*"

Peter, tired, drained, suffering from complete and utter exhaustion, dropped the handgun to his side and laid it on the nightstand next to where the captain was working on his friend. He stood there silent, in surrender, ready to be arrested.

"Pete, what the hell? What are you doing in here?" a grimy Joey Cipriano bellowed from the tent doorway. He assessed the situation quickly as an MP brushed him aside, heading to place Peter under arrest.

The entire tent full of wounded soldiers was now silently absorbed in watching the drama unfold.

"Hey, man, what you doin' with my buddy?" he asked, walking up to the MP who had Peter by the arm, quickly assisted by another MP arriving seconds later.

"Back off, soldier, or we'll arrest you, too," one of the MP's commanded as they awaited the medical officer to press formal charges. The doctor was still working on Clamser.

"My God, he's alive," he said. "Don't know how long he'll last, but this man definitely wants to live," the doctor offered as he shot the watery solution into Clamser's chest.

The doctor turned to the nightstand and picked up the .45, examining it. "No ammo clip?" he asked Peter.

Peter's expression questioned the doctor. "Yes, sir. It's always loaded," he answered. "Always," he sighed, eyes questioning—looking for the clip.

The captain held the grip end up to show the ragged, tired corporal that there was no clip. "Why?" the doctor asked simply, still handling the weapon with curiosity.

"He's . . . my friend," came a haltingly direct answer. Joey looked on then moved in.

"Sir, I think I can explain." The two MP's scowled, seeking to block him from the bedside where the drama was being acted out.

"Let him by," the doctor ordered.

"Sir, we've been at the front continuously since landing here in North Africa in October. We were in the lead platoon at Kasserine. We got our tank shot out from underneath us. Corporal O'Banyon, he's a damn hero, sir. He should get a medal for what he did. The enemy wasn't one hundred meters away, blowing our guys to bits, and Pete, I mean Corporal O'Banyon here, hell, he ran out there with all this heavy armor firing at us, German infantry on our heels, and picks up this dying sergeant of ours. I thought, no way he's gonna make it, but he did. Then we drove in full retreat for three nights straight. We had dumped Clamser off—the guy in the bed there—with an ambulance near the front. I thought sure as hell he was dead.

"We haven't eaten, slept, cleaned up. . . . We came straight here looking for our sergeant. And that's the truth. Can't ya see—"

The captain cut him off. "Corporal, you should be court-martialed. I see no harm, however, in an empty gun used as influence in saving a man's life. If I weren't in the business of life saving . . . well, get out of here before I change my mind." He handed the weapon to Peter who holstered it. The MP's released their grip.

"You sure you don't want to press charges?" asked the MP with stripes on his sleeve.

The doctor nodded.

"Will he make it?" Peter mumbled, moisture running down his dirt-caked cheeks and smearing the grime further into a face already soiled beyond recognition.

"Come back tomorrow. There are no guarantees. But this man has an extraordinary will to live."

Joey thanked the medical officer quietly and tugged at Peter, leading him to the tent exit. "I borrowed your last ammo clip yesterday, you lucky S-O-B."

Applause from the wounded in the tentlike hall, made sacred by the devotion shown by one comrade for another, increased in intensity.

The handclapping started first with one soldier, then another, and another until a crescendo of applause rolled through the hospital tent like thunder. Just as the singing of the Fred Astaire song had moments earlier, the soldiers found a new affirmation in which to engage themselves. More somber than the playful singing, louder than the music that had blared from the box radio, solemn like the reverence given to Sunday Mass, yet triumphant. They applauded the broken and tired soldier who dared risk his freedom for a fallen comrade.

Peter offered a tired salute to the soldiers, walked back to the radio, and turned it on. Then, like a marionette's puppet with broken strings, his youthful body, worn thin and shaken from battle and three sleepless nights of retreat, collapsed into Joey's arms.

"My turn," Joey said as he put his arms around his tankmate and dragged the sunken young hero to the tent door.

25

ANNA READ the headlines. The battle was already one week in the past. The war correspondent Ernie Pyle broached the American defeat with a crisp but no-nonsense look at how the American troops responded to an overwhelming, German, armored counterattack in the Tunisian desert at a place called Kasserine Pass.

Uncle Billie was awake.

"Anna, darlin', what does it say about the war? Does it say anything about our lad and his boys?"

"Yes," she swallowed, choking back the saltiness, blinking it clear from her eyes. "It says . . . ah, it says, American First Armored Division bloodied in their first taste of battle with German Panzer units." She put the newspaper down and went to Billie unashamed, laying her head against his chest, tearful, brokenhearted, afraid.

He stroked her crimson locks gently, carefully, fatherly, and closed his eyes, grateful to be able to offer something to her, something for the kindness he had needed in his aloneness.

Although he could not be sure, he sensed Peter was yet alive and that surely God would not abandon the O'Banyon clan now, not after seeing it almost destroyed from the earth. Surely God would not allow Peter to be butchered like so many lambs in the cruelty of war.

"He's alive darlin'. I'm sure of it," he finally offered.

"He is? Really?" Anna queried, clearing her eyes like a toddler awakening from sleep. "Are you sure?"

"Aye."

"Oh, Uncle Billie. You are a sweet man. Somehow if you say so then I believe."

He smiled. "Your happiness is healing me . . . your gentle ways, like Katie." He looked away embarrassed.

"Oh, you wonderful man," Anna said bending over the bed to give him a kiss.

"Could ya read the article? Now we know Peter made it an' all, I think we should hear what he's goin' through."

Anna cleared her throat and began to read Ernie Pyle's exact words.

SOMEWHERE IN NORTH AFRICA

Well, our boys suffered the bitter taste of defeat as they came up against the angry and battle-hardened forces of Field Marshall Erwin Rommel's experienced Panzer divisions at a place called Kasserine Pass.

By now telegrams void of facts on how their boys died will be arriving to thousands of American homes. This is not a column I want to write but in fairness to our fighting men out here in the desert and to our fallen comrades, I feel I must.

You see, you might well get the wrong idea of our boys unless you hear it from one who was there.

You'd be real proud of your sons, brothers, husbands, fathers. They stood up against the finest of the Nazi Third Reich—men who have been at war for three years, and didn't yield ground without inflicting a heavy penalty on the enemy.

The surprise attack on our Infantry and Armored Divisions at Kasserine was something the boys already have learned from and will make them better fighting men. The lessons learned here will be employed over and over again as we renew our battle against Hitler's war machine.

The following has been written for my book about your hero sons here in North Africa. The book titled Here Is Your War *tells it like I see it and live it every day. I think you should know a little what it's like for our men, so here goes. The following actions occurred days previous and led to the rout we experienced at Kasserine Pass in a desert locale called Sidi bou Zid:*

"We looked, and could see through our glasses the enemy advancing. They were far away, perhaps ten miles—narrow little streaks of dust, like plumes, speeding down the low-sloping plain from the mountain base toward the oasis of Sidi bou Zid. We could not see the German tanks, only dust plumes extending and pushing forward.

"Just then I realized we were standing on the very hill the general had picked out for me on his map that morning. It was not good enough. I said to the young lieutenant, "Let's get on up there."

" 'I'm ready,' he replied.

"So we got into the jeep, and went leaping and bounding up toward what was—but we didn't know it then—the

most ghastly armored melee that had occurred until then in Tunisia.

"It was odd, the way we went up into the thick of the battle in our jeep. We didn't attach ourselves to anybody. We didn't ask for permission to go. We just started the motor and went. Vehicles ahead of us had worn a sort of track across the desert and through irrigated fields. We followed that for awhile, keeping our place in the forward-moving procession. We were just a jeep with two brown-clad figures in it, indistinguishable from the rest.

"The line was moving cautiously. Every now and then the procession would stop. A few times we stopped, too. We shut off our motor to listen for planes. But, finally, we tired of the slow progress. We dashed out across the sand and the Arabs' plowed fields, skirting cactus fences and small farmyards. As we did this, a sensation of anxiety—which had not touched me before—came over me. It was a fear of mines in the freshly dug earth; one touch of a wheel and we could easily be blown into little bits. I spoke of this to the lieutenant, but he said he didn't think they had had time to plant mines. I thought to myself, "Hell, it doesn't take all night to plant a mine.'

"We did not—it is obvious to report—hit any mines.

"The battlefield was an incongruous thing. Always there was some ridiculous impingement of normalcy on a field of battle. There on that day it was the Arabs. They were herding their camels, just as usual. Some of them continued to plow their fields. Children walked along, driving their sack-laden burros, as tanks and guns clanked past them. The sky was filled with planes and smoke burst from screaming shells.

"As we smashed along over a field of new grain, which pushed its small shoots just a few inches above the earth, the *asinine thought popped into my head: I wonder if the army got permission to use this land before starting the attack.*

"Both sides had crossed and recrossed those farms in the past twenty-four hours. The fields were riddled by deep ruts and by wide spooky tracks of the almost mythical Mark VI. Evidence of the previous day's battle was still strewn across the desert. We passed charred half-tracks. We stopped to look into a burned-out tank, named Texas, from which a lieutenant-colonel friend of mine and his crew had demolished four German tanks before being put out of commission themselves.

"We passed a trailer still full of American ammunition, which had been abandoned. . . .

"We moved on closer to the actual tank battle ahead, but never went right into it—for in a jeep that would have been a fantastic form of suicide. We stopped, I should judge, about a mile behind the foremost tanks.

"Behind us the desert was still alive with men and machines moving up. Later we learned some German tanks had maneuvered in behind us, and were shooting up our half-tracks and jeeps. But fortunately we didn't know that at the time.

"Light American tanks came up from the rear and stopped near us. They were to be held there in reserve, in case they had to be called into the game in this league which was much too heavy and hot for them. Their crews jumped out the moment they stopped, and began digging foxholes against the inevitable arrival of the dive bombers.

"Soon the dive bombers came. They set fires behind us. American and German tanks were burning ahead of us. Our planes came over, too, strafing and bombing the enemy.

"One of our half-tracks, full of ammunition, was livid

red, with flames leaping and swaying. Every few seconds one of its shells would go off, and the projectile would tear into the sky with a weird whang-zing sort of noise. Field artillery had stopped just on our right. They began shelling the German artillery beyond our tanks. It didn't take long for the German artillery to answer.

"The scream of an approaching shell is an appalling thing. We could hear them coming. Then we could see the dust kick up a couple of hundred yards away. The shells hit the ground and ricocheted like armor-piercing shells, which did not explode but skip along the ground until they finally lose momentum or hit something.

"War has its own peculiar sounds. They are not really very much different from the sounds in the world of peace. But they clothe themselves in an unforgettable fierceness, just because born in danger and death."

Anna couldn't continue reading. The chill of the first-person account was something she had never read or heard before. Peter never talked about this kind of danger in his letters.

"Ya can't go on, can ya lass?" Uncle Billie announced sullenly. "I understand, I don't think I can bear much more of it myself, though I do want ta know what my boy is going through."

"I'll clip it out, and we'll save these Ernie Pyle stories for when we feel up to it," she said, wiping at the sniffles that were now under control.

"That will be grand. Maybe Peter can read them and tell us all about them when he returns."

"I would like that much better," Anna answered. "Are you ready for my mother's famous New England beef stew with extra onions?" Anna smiled, helping Uncle Billie sit on the edge of the bed.

"Oh, how I love your home cookin'," he smiled. "Ya hear that, Laddie? Beef stew," he said patting his sheepdog gently. Laddie let go with a quiet whine and wag of his tail. "I'm feelin' much better, ya know," he added as he walked slowly to the small dining table situated in the corner of the kitchen with its large picture windows overlooking the bay.

"You're not ready for the lamp lighting yet," Anna smiled, dishing out the thick, meaty porridge to the lighthouse keeper.

He reached gently for her hand. "Our Gracious Heavenly Father, we give humble thanks for our portion of life-givin' nourishment this day. We are mindful of the awful war and destruction this country is engaged in, especially our Peter. We ask thee ta bless and protect our Peter from enemy harm. Make him valiant, strong, and full of firmness in this just cause. To you who lights each man's path, light ours and light Peter's. Make us ever comforted in this hour of fear and trial of faith. In the name of the Holy One, Jesus. Amen."

"Thank you, Uncle Billie," Anna responded quietly. A solemn hush had come over the meal and table setting until Uncle Billie spoke to her.

"Peter will be feasting with ya right here at this table in no time. You and the wee ones will never be without. I promise ya."

She smiled and dipped a portion of bread into the stew. She finally nodded as if she believed what he had just said.

"That's my girl. Trust this old lightkeeper."

26

PETER AND Joey gathered around the supply truck with the same anxious stare in their eyes that made every soldier in their company look alike. They were hungry for mail, any word from home to help them cope with the insanity of the desert war.

"Peters," the master sergeant called out.

"Here," responded two soldiers in unison.

"Hold your horses, O'Banyon. I said Peters, not Peter," the sergeant stated. "Johnson . . . O'Hare . . . Smith, J. B . . . Smith Charles, E . . . Patterson . . . Boswell . . . Maguire . . . Martinez . . . Jones Henry, A . . . Jones, William . . . Cipriano."

Joey eagerly moved through the crowd, picked up his letter, and kissed it, moving off to the bed of a nearby truck to be alone with it.

"Powell . . . Kendal . . . Forrest . . . Murphy . . . Adams . . . Burt . . ." the sergeant called out. The letters were handed over the heads to soldiers calling, "Here!"

"Gordon . . . Llewellen . . . Miller, David . . . Miller, John . . . MacGregor . . . Johnson again . . . Martinez again . . . Cipriano . . . I said Cipriano," the sergeant called out louder as Joey scrambled back to pick up his letter. "O'Banyon . . . That's it for today, girls," the sergeant gruffly mocked to the grumbling of soldiers who walked away empty-handed.

Peter eagerly took the letter and sat down under the shade of an old, gnarled olive tree, propping himself up against one side while two other soldiers shared the thick and stumpy trunk on opposite sides.

He tore open the envelope carefully and began to read.

Peter darling,

I am writing this letter from the lighthouse. I am here taking care of Uncle Billie who didn't want me to tell you, but I feel I should. He had a sudden heart attack, Hal found him on the floor in pain, and I came, first to the hospital on Nantucket where he recuperated, and then Hal and I brought him home here to the lighthouse.

I'm keeping the light on for you, darling. Uncle Billie looks good, and I think will be fine. There is much too much fight in him I think. He hates bed rest and tries to get up to do the duties around here, but I won't let him. He's met his stubborn match.

He told me to tell you he loves you and prays for you each day. I know he does, because I hear him. He is so sweet and gentle. I now know where his nephew got all those wonderful qualities.

We read the account of the battle at Kasserine Pass. Ernie Pyle writes a weekly column. I cut out every one of them and wonder as he describes the scenery, the battles, and talks of

148

tanks and things if he isn't describing you and what you are going through.

It is hard to read and then wonder if you are okay. I can't believe that you are engaged in the awful business of shooting and being shot at. I can't imagine it at all.

I just pray morning, afternoon, and evening for your safety. Please be careful and come home to me, darling. I would be lost without you. Uh, oh. Here goes hanky time again.

Well, I must be lighting the lamp upstairs now. I love you, darling. I go to the pier and wait for you as if you were home, and coming there to be with me like you used to do after you finished getting the chores done at the lighthouse. It gives me comfort there.

I dream of you, me, our children, and this place. I am forever yours.

With all my love, darling
Anna

Peter held the letter up to smell her presence there. It was perfumed, and with eyes closed, it was almost like touching her soft cheeks, running his fingers through her silky, crimson locks, being in her embrace.

"Hey, Pete, get a load of this. This letter from my sister says Eisenhower hinted we could all be home by Christmas. What do you think?"

Peter grinned. "So the Nazis are afraid of us. They want to make peace?"

"She says the Army Air Corps is bombing the hell out of Germany, the Japs, too. I guess people are pretty upbeat back home."

"Even though we got whipped?"

"She says the papers called it a gallant stand at a desert wadi called Kasserine Pass in Tunisia. The papers call it our 'initiation rites,'" Joey laughed. "Initiation . . . gallant stand? Don't see as the German's gave us much choice."

Peter's eyes smiled in contempt. "They say we're going to get a new tank and a couple of new guys. One of those M4 Medium Sherman jobs."

"Says who?" Joey asked as he nudged Peter to give himself some room to sit down under the tree.

"Company brass. Captain Joslin. Today, maybe tomorrow."

"You know what I think?"

"No, what do you think, Joey?"

"I think you is gonna be the new tank commander. Three stripes and all."

"What makes you think so?"

"Everybody knows what you did for Clamser back there at Kasserine and then at the hospital. . . . There's talk of you being put in for the big one." Joey smiled broadly and jabbed his partner.

"Get out a here," Peter shoved back.

"You just wait and see. My ten to your five and these three fresh farm eggs I bought from an Arab this morning says that I'm right." He opened a handkerchief that contained three carefully wrapped, brown-colored chicken eggs.

"You're on."

"Guess I'm gonna have to teach you a lesson about gambling," Joey smiled. "Come on. The lunch wagon," he nudged Peter. "Hot food. Man, I can't believe these rear-echelon guys eat so good."

27

H ER TOES dipped into the chilly Atlantic water. A shawl protected her from a brisk but unusually temperate February breeze. The sun was rising though and warmed her enough.

She held her shawl out over her shoulders and, letting it sail in the wind, took the morning sun in. Then, slowly, she wrapped her arms together as if she were including someone in them.

Dancing lightly upon the pier, as she had a thousand times, she hummed the tune Dorothy sang in the Wizard of Oz. "Somewhere over the rainbow . . ." she voiced and hummed and waltzed playfully as though her cares could be blown away to wherever the breeze wisping upon her brow went.

North? East? West? The breeze could gently carry her worries away, and she would be with Peter again soon. He had always watched her little dance from atop the hill and then joined her here, she thought.

Her pink cotton dress swayed and swirled in the soothing

offshore puffs of winter air as she tiptoed upon the wooden planks. The faint lapping against the pilings was like applause from an unseen audience who approved of cheerfulness, of her overcoming fears carried deep inside her.

Pulling her shawl around her, she stopped and sat upon the end of the pier and stared into the depth of the water. She could almost hear his laugh, his tame teasing. His whisper in her ear tickled when he said, "I love you, baby."

Anna held a hand over her middle. She had part of him there. Barely showing now, their child was living proof that love can live on.

If Peter dies in war, could I ever love again? Would I want to? She posed the silent question and answered it in her heart.

"Hello, lass," the deep bass voice of Uncle Billie soothed. "Stay, stay," he motioned to Anna and sat down next to her. He noticed her attempt to hide her swollen eyes.

"I know, I know. I shouldn't be climbing up and down these beach stairs from the lighthouse," he smiled as he sat next to her on the wood planks. "I might as well die trying to live a little as die in bed waitin' ta get better," he smiled.

Anna nodded, smiled, and then leaned up against the old man. She needed strength and his was real and reassuring, like her grandfather who would nuzzle her upon her cheek with his bearded face when she was a little girl. Now, Billie's soft gray whiskers found themselves against her head as he tenderly cradled her.

"Ah, Anna lass. Do you know why I became a lighthouse keeper?" he asked as she sniffled and wiped at her eyes. She shook her head.

"I know a little bit about why you came here . . . about Katie and your little boy. Peter told me in a letter," she finally replied.

"Ah, then ya know that I was a lonely man. Except for Peter's father, Phillip, I had no one . . . no one at all ta call family."

"It must have been hard," she responded.

"Harder than a soul could bear, it seems. There were many days when I wanted to end it all for the pain in my heart."

"You, Uncle Billie? But you are so strong. You wouldn't have," Anna said surprised.

"I could've, but didn't. I don't suppose there isn't a sorrow, temptation, or emotion I haven't gone through these twenty-four years since my boy and Katie left me." He gazed far beyond the line that marked where sea and sky met. "I was an angry man for quite awhile."

"I'm angry," Anna voiced softly.

"Aye. I know ya are."

"I hate this war. I hate to think of men killing each other. I hate the stupidity of Hitler and his leaders. It's always the old men who start it. Why don't they fight each other? The generals, I mean?"

"Aye," he answered in agreement.

"Why? Why should boys . . . young men die?"

"They shouldn't."

"Well, why don't we all just say no and . . . and . . . oh, I don't know." She got up and walked around the edge of the pier. "I don't want Peter to die, Uncle Billie," she pleaded and sat back down next to him as he tried to sort out what part of the big picture he could share, the reasons for living he had been given, something that might give her solace.

"Anna, lass. Ya got time for a little story tellin'?" he asked, looking down into her sad blue eyes.

She nodded.

"Well, then, maybe if I can tell ya about how this place

changed me and something more, ya can find some answer to your question."

She nodded again.

"After it all happened, I felt lost, and I was wanderin' through the southern part of Manhattan and somehow found myself in St. Peter's Cathedral. I looked up at the altar and then at the image of the crucified Christ and wondered *why*— and this was the first time I ever thought it, mind you—*why* the church always had him hanging on the cross and not breakin' out o' the tomb. . . . Death, you know, was on my mind.

"A strange thought it was. *Why,* I asked myself, *couldn't we put a chain around our necks with, instead of the crucifix, a rock with beams of light coming out of it to remind us he didn't just die but promised everlastin' life?* I wasn't meanin' to be sacrilegious with these new thoughts of mine. It was just that it wasn't how my mind's eye was seeing things. All of a sudden I had this thought, *Didn't he break out of the tomb Easter morn? Isn't he a livin' Christ? Not a dyin' one?*

"Hope is a powerful elixir for what ails the soul. Suddenly I was thinkin' in terms of this hope of life after death. You know, I wasn't what I would exactly call religious, but I did believe. I just wasn't as sure as my Katie was. But I always liked the part in the holy book when the good Lord appeared, after his death, to the disciples in the same upper room where he had eaten the last supper with them.

"It just seemed fittin', ya know, that he being the first one to live after dyin' should go there, resurrected is what the good book calls it, to the place where he broke the bread and drank the wine with them three days before.

"Now, I'm still not too religious, but I felt a spark of spirit that day as I thought it in the dark cathedral lit up with just candles. I guess being religious means goin' ta Mass, doing symbolic things, and bein' spiritual means livin' it.

"Bein' so far from cathedrals and churches and such, I can't say I really ever got religious, but I drew closer to Him, precept upon precept, as I learned 'em."

Silence . . . a pause . . . and both storyteller and listener looked out to sea.

"Uncle Billie?"

"Yes, lass?"

"Is that the whole story?"

"Oh, no . . . I just stopped ta think is all."

More silence followed as they both eyed the gulls soaring high on the wind currents. It was early in the day still. The ocean hadn't churned up enough for the gulls to squabble over.

He began again. "Ya know who Jesus showed himself first to after risin' from the dead?"

"Mary, the woman who he forgave and then the other women, Martha and his Mother," she proudly responded like a child in Sunday School to the teacher.

"Aye! Aye, that's it! He showed himself to the loves in his life. His livin', breathin', lovin' women who treated him so well in life. They had been devoted to him, and he showed them this respect. Then he showed himself to his other followers, the disciples.

"Life and death . . . that was what hit me that day long ago. Like the sea here. It is a constant. For one to live, one must die. But my Katie dying, leavin' me? I still couldn't see it.

"I left the Cathedral with a new idea though and couldn't for the life of me get it out of my head. Christ!

"I was mad at him moments before. Now I wondered not at his image on the cross but his comin' from the tomb."

"Uncle Billie, that painting?" Anna perked up. "Over the old ship's clock on the mantle? Is that . . . ?"

His eyes twinkled. "Aye. That would be the image in my mind. Given to me by Father Shannon in Ireland at the death of my Da. I'd stowed it away never thinkin' to bring it out. But I finally did."

Anna leaned her head against him again, trying to comprehend where he was heading with this. But it was comforting to hear his story of overcoming sorrow. She quietly waited for him to begin again.

"Anyway, I walked for all the while thinkin', thinkin', all the time thinkin' and was headed to the place I first met Katie in Central Park years before. I had always gone there after Mass on my day off from work to write to my kin and think o' home. Now, I went there regular to try to be near that happy memory when I first gazed into the loveliest azure eyes I've ever known.

"And thinkin' all the time of this light, the image in my mind of the Christ, not dyin', but ya know, comin' out o' the tomb, and the glorious light. I couldn't get it out o' my mind and didn't even know why I was happy—feelin' happy in spite of Katie and the lad—like I'd found a secret. Ya know what I'm tryin' ta say?"

Anna looked up into eyes she had never seen wet before.

"Anyway, I got to Central Park and went to the old bench by the lake and sat ponderin' on this singular occurrence, this epiphany that came to me in the cathedral. As I sat there thinkin' about bein' so alone but also full of strange new hope ta see Katie and my wee darlin' lad again, up walks this man out from nowhere it seemed and hands me this pocketbook and says, 'If ya never read another book, read this one. It's a best seller. It'll change yer life.' "

Billie pulled out a tattered and worn pocket Bible from his overalls and began to finger smudged pages.

"As I live an breathe, Anna, the book opened to this passage, 'I am the light of the world: he that followeth me shall not walk in darkness, but shall have the light of life.' Right there, reading that twelfth verse in the eighth chapter of St. John, I knew someone was tryin' ta tell me I'd be okay and see my darlin's once more. I looked for the man ta thank him, but he was gone.

"It wasn't one week later that this lighthouse was offered me by my employer down at the wharf, and I knew that I should come, be here, spend my time giving light to those on troubled seas, waitin' for Katie to come back to me.

"I built this very pier yer sittin' on, plank by plank, piling after piling, with these two hands," he said, holding them up.

"I built the small bungalow attached to the lighthouse tower, too. I did it all for my lady and the wee one.

"I did it all to the glory of God for takin' my miserable life and showin' me the good path—I haven't always been an angel, bein' a sailor and all—but Katie, she started takin' the rough edges off, then God finished the job.

"I've been waitin' a thousand times at dusk, on the end of this old pier, lookin' out to sea, waitin' for my Katie to come back from her watery depths. Simon Peter walked on water to meet the risen Jesus on the stormy waters of the Galilee two thousand years ago. If I see her comin', I'll walk right off and meet her there. I know it sure as I'm William Robert O'Banyon. Ya know what I'm trying ta say to you . . . about never givin' up, about hope?"

"You sweet man, I'm not sure I know what you are trying to say, but it felt good and that's enough for me. You are going to get some of my seafood chowder in a bowl for lunch. Shall we?" Anna stood and held out her arm.

He bowed in respect, taking his cap off. "My lady, I would be honored to escort you to the Chowder Ball."

"That's *chowder* in a *bowl,*" she laughed.

He winked at her, obviously delighted at having found her on the pier, at the edge of sorrow, now full of joy and so very full of love.

28

GENERAL GEORGE S. Patton, new commander of the Second Corps in northern Africa, having arrived that very day from allied headquarters in Casablanca, eyed the tanks and their crews lined up for inspection, row by row, then began a short and direct speech on the state of affairs in Tunisia and how he intended to change things.

Sergeant Peter O'Banyon, his crew, and several other tank commanders and crews took front line as they stood outside each tank respectfully. The platform Patton stood on was no more than twenty feet in front of them.

After some introductory pleasantries, General Patton launched into his monologue to Combat Command B of the First Armored Division.

"I have recently been assigned by General Eisenhower to shape you into a real fighting force. You and I will get along fine as long as you are killing Germans.

"I anticipate once that is accomplished, to the point that they are either all dead or captured in Northern Africa, I will go back to Casablanca and continue to engage in strategic planning operations to take the war to Hitler's own back yard.

"In case you have any ideas about taking it easy, you might as well get that out of your heads now. I am here to fight and to win. That is all. The sooner you fight and win with me, the sooner you may be rid of me.

"You men who have just tasted battle against Rommel's finest Panzer units have retreated for the last time in this war. You are to stand and fight and, by damn, die like men before you allow them kraut-fed, illegitimate sons of Hun canines to make you retreat and lose one lousy inch of this fine Arab soil!

"You have one standing order. That is attack, attack, attack! Dammit all, men, they can't attack you if you're the ones taking the initiative! The harder we push, the more Nazis we kill. The more Nazis we kill, the fewer Americans will die.

"We will attack at night, at dawn, in broad daylight. We will be ruthless, show no mercy, and overcome all obstacles.

"Further, I have inspected several outfits in the Second Corps. You all have been a disgrace to the uniforms you wear. This isn't some desert picnic, some casual affair. We are United States soldiers fighting against tank forces hardened in battle for two and one-half years!

"I will not have any of my men die or become captured, looking like some ragtag bunch of Army losers from some reserve outfit who just finished a crap game on their furlough."

Peter grinned, knowing Joey must be loving this.

"No, sir," Patton continued. "From now on, you will dress in full leggings; you will each wear the authorized U.S. Army combat helmets, at all times. And for you tankers, the Army-issued head gear, overalls, and webbing, and you will wear ties under your battle fatigues until we push that Nazi Party loving, second-class tank commander, Field Marshal Rommel, into the Mediterranean Sea!" he screamed in his inborn, high-pitched voice, so unlike his stern-and-hard manly exterior, pacing while he walked the platform.

"Part of the trouble with this outfit is that you've had no discipline up until now. War is won by discipline and by killing more of those bastards than they can kill of you! It's no wonder you got your asses kicked at Kasserine Pass.

"Well, no more, dammit! You will act, dress, and behave like America's finest fighting men, and if you die, then you'll already be dressed appropriately to meet St. Peter. Am I understood?" he snapped, wacking the railing of the platform with his swagger stick.

"Yes, sir!" the brigade yelled in unison.

"Good. Now I'll take some time for decorations for some of you men who held your ground like true soldiers at Kasserine. And then," he added, "we are going after that SOB Rommel and kick his sorry hind-end out of Kasserine!"

He strode down the steps of the platform and headed for the lead tank in the row awaiting the general's inspection, his staff in tow.

"Major, the first commendation, please," Patton ordered.

"Private First Class Joseph Cipriano promoted to corporal and to be awarded the following: the Bronze Star for bravery in the field of battle against lead elements of the Nazi counterattack at Kasserine Pass. Private Cipriano drove an abandoned supply truck in the face of intense enemy fire to rescue surrounded comrades. Corporal Joseph Cipriano. The Bronze Star."

"Congratulations, Corporal. How many Nazis did you kill?" Patton asked sternly.

"I don't recall, sir. I'll count next time," Joey smiled.

"Good. Good man," Patton chuckled as he moved on. "Oh . . . Cipriano was it?"

"Yes, sir."

"What were you doing driving a truck? Don't you drive tanks? Did you lose your tank or something?"

"Well, not exactly, sir. See the Germans shot it up and—"

"Don't let it happen again," Patton interrupted. "Those are expensive pieces of equipment, soldier. We didn't train you to drive six-cylinder, duce-and-a-half supply trucks."

"Yes, sir."

The major read again as they moved on. "Corporal Peter O'Banyon promoted to the rank of sergeant and tank commander following the battle of Kasserine Pass. In the face of approaching enemy infantry and tanks, he abandoned his position of safety and yielded himself to hostile fire over open terrain to come to the aid of his seriously wounded tank commander. Because of this action, the life of a soldier was spared. Sergeant Peter O'Banyon. The Silver Star."

"Congratulations, Sergeant," Patton offered as he hung the medal around his neck. "How many of those Nazi bastards did you kill?" General Patton asked, squinting in eyeball-to-eyeball contact with the stiffly standing, erect, and at-attention sergeant.

"Not enough, sir," Peter said without looking into the eyes of the general.

"Good answer. I like that," Patton said commending him as he stood facing Peter, hands on each of his ivory-handled revolvers.

"We've got a major battle coming up. We're going to send that Hitler-lovin' bastard Rommel home to Berlin with his tail between his legs, if I don't capture him first. How would you like to be lead tank?"

"Say when, sir," Peter replied smartly.

"Major, remind me to take a look at this man's file. He may just be our first soldier in the First Armored to earn the big one."

The major continued until he and General Patton had awarded medals for bravery to one-dozen soldiers, and the brigade was dismissed.

"Well, that's just swell. Real swell. What were you thinking, Pete? Patton says, 'How would you like to be lead tank in the next battle?' Sergeant O'Banyon says, 'Just say when, sir.' Hell, Pete, if you're lead tank commander, then I've got only one choice," Joey said as they both climbed up on the Sherman M4.

"What's that?" Pete replied, taking in the unusually serious Joey.

Joey pushed his index finger into Pete's chest. "Pray to God you really are a good-luck charm; otherwise, we are dead men. You know any lead tanker still alive in our outfit?"

Peter looked at him in silence. What was he supposed to say to the general? Peter had no good answer, really.

They paused, staring at each other.

"I've got a lighthouse to go home to. A woman and a kid. I'm goin' home to them. You just drive like the *lucky* Italian crapshooter you are." The new crew members, Miller and Olson, were already inside.

"I'll drive like you've never seen before. Just don't let this hero crap go to your head."

"Look, Joey, I'd rather be a live hero than a sergeant with command of this tank. But since I am commander, you just drive real good and make my decisions easy," Peter answered seriously.

"Yes, sir! I'll make sure I don't lose another tank, sir! Mighty expensive equipment, sir!" Joey saluted sarcastically.

"Awe, knock it off and get this Panzer killer going before I make one of the new guys driver and make you the gunloader."

"He gets another stripe and thinks he's the Almighty himself," Joey mockingly grinned.

29

ANNA LOOKED surprised as she opened the door to find Hal from the Port Hope ferry docks. He had a small package in his hand and stood facing the cove.

"Yes?" she asked nervously to Hal's back.

"Oh, hello, Anna. How's Billie?" he asked, turning, a somber expression written on his face.

"He's right here. Come in," she answered politely, eyeing the package in his hand.

"Actually, I came with this for you. Just arrived in today's mail shipment from Nantucket."

Anna cocked her head sideways and looked at the brown paper-wrapped box that fit easily in the palm of her hand.

"It's from Peter," she smiled happily.

Hal shuffled his feet anxiously, with head bent, as she sat down and gently but quickly opened it. It was a small black box. Square. She undid the lid.

"Oh, my. Uncle Billie?" she called.

"I'm comin', darlin'," he answered as he slowly descended the steps from the lighthouse.

"Hello, Billie," Hal said somberly.

"What has put ya in such a fine mood, Hal? The old lady kick ya out again for drinkin'?" Billie laughed at his own remark.

Hal just nodded to Anna who was examining the military decoration and a note from her husband.

"Says here General George S. Patton himself pinned it on him. And Joey got one, too, for bravery at Kasserine Pass." Anna smiled, handing the medal to Billie.

"Awe, there now. What did I tell ya, darlin'? Peter is bein' looked out for by his guardian angel. No doubt."

Hal swallowed hard and cleared his throat.

"Anything the matter, Hal?" Anna asked, smiling. Her eyes met a look of concern reflected in the harbor master's face. Her natural upturned crease of the lips pouted with the questioning look of someone being offered unexpected, unwanted news.

"I, uh, just got the latest edition of the *Boston Globe*." He pulled it out of his back pocket. The headline "Patton Pushes Nazi's Back" caught Anna and Billie's immediate attention.

Anna read quickly through the article, aloud for the benefit of Billie:

NEAR GAFSA, TUNISIA

Combined forces of the American Second Corps lead by the First Armored Division engaged the Axis forces for the first time since their stunning defeat at Kasserine Pass last month.

Sources at the front say that while the battle has begun to turn in favor of the American tanks and infantry, the retreating Germans, in their stubborn bid to retain control of Tunisia, their last foothold on the African continent, caused moderate to heavy losses to our boys.

General George S. Patton, the no-nonsense tank soldier, personally lead the attack at two crossroads by the names of Gafsa and Maknassy in the Tunisian desert.

The Americans appear victorious with the British Eighth and Second Armies pouring it on the Nazi's from north and south of the Americans. The command of Erwin Rommel, better known as the "Desert Fox," cannot hold out long. Although the Germans still hold the ports at Bizerte and Tunis, the Allied Air Corps has been making daily bombing runs, causing widespread damage to port facilities and Axis airfields nearby. This breaking up of any chances the Germans might have of resupply or escape by sea almost certainly seals their doom.

Adolph Hitler himself has given the German High Command in Tunisia one order. They are to "fight to the last man."

More information forthcoming as we receive updates from the front.

Anna looked at the letter that came in the small box with the military medal, the Silver Star, and read it.

My darling Anna,

By now you may have read in the papers about General Patton being new commander of the Second Corps here in Africa. Enclosed is an award I got for helping one of our guys at Kasserine Pass. Believe me, I wasn't thinking of being a hero. It's just that this guy, Sergeant Clamser, had a wife and a couple of kids, and I knew he would've done the same for me.

I guess I got an angel on my shoulder like Uncle Billie promised—that and a crazy Italian driver, Joey, who pitched in and got us all out of there okay. He was awarded the Bronze Star.

They call General Patton "Old Blood and Guts" on account of his approach to warfare—attack! But I didn't expect anything else out of this. You shouldn't worry. I feel like I'll get out of this okay.

I've got to go. Give my love to Uncle Billie. Take care of yourself and our baby.

I love you darling.

Your husband forever,
Pete

"He sounds okay here in the letter," Anna said to Billie and Hal, trying to reassure herself.

"Billie, Anna. Maybe you should sit down." Hal motioned for them to sit on the sofa.

"Hal? What's wrong? What are you holding back?" Anna asked, tearing up.

"Hal, what would ya be holdin' on to? Let us have it now," Billie added.

Hal pulled out a yellow onion-skinned envelope from his coat pocket. "This just came in, Anna," he said apologetically. "I'm not sure what it'll say. I pray for you both," Hal said stiffly, with a sniffle, as he handed the telegram into Anna's trembling hands.

She stared at it in disbelief. Her brave attempts to maintain composure and acceptance didn't temper the deep feeling of tragedy looming as she broke the envelope's seal.

"I can't do this, Uncle Billie," she shrugged as she mopped the moisture away with the back of her hand. "Please. You open it for me," she asked as the seasoned seafarer put his arms around her.

He took it from her hands as she rested her head against his sagging but voluminous, barrel-chested frame. Billie broke the seal carefully and began to read:

"I'm okay . . . stop . . . Slightly wounded . . . stop . . . In field hospital . . . stop . . . Don't want army telegram to get there first, worry you . . . stop . . . Friend sending this for me . . . stop . . . Joey okay too . . . stop . . . With me . . . stop . . . Not hurt bad . . . stop . . . Will be as good as new . . . stop . . . Get medal? . . . stop . . . I love you. Pete.

"I love you too, darling! Oh, I love you, too!"

Anna held the telegram to her breast while the two grown men looked up at the ceiling as if it offered a sure and sudden remedy for the loss of composure sweeping over them.

One man, Uncle Billie, who choked back the saltiness beading under his weathered eyes, gazed away from the other, Hal, now relieved at the news he had been bearer of. Both sought a balm for the emotion that had so quickly broken through their manly emotional command but without avail, as Billie wept quietly, unashamedly with his nephew's wife.

No greater balm came, nor was needed, than the knowledge their boy was alive.

30

S OME RIDE we all had in the lead tank," Private Miller crowed sarcastically as Joey dealt cards on his bed. Next to him lay Pete, asleep, with his arm in a sling and leg in splints.

"What are you griping about? You ain't dead. Got a sore head, a few stiches is all," Joey responded. "Hell. Look at Olsen. He ain't never gonna be the same," Joey pointed to the bed across the aisle. "Private Olsen minus one leg. Ticket home but he ain't goin' skiing no more. Where the hell he say he was from?"

"Iowa," Miller said apologetically. "I didn't mean to—"

"Don't say nothin'. You ain't got no right to bitch until you been here for a few battles. Then you can complain."

"Who's complaining?" Miller shot back and then, comprehending the look in Joey's eyes, decided to take his hand and play it.

"You gonna take a card or just sit there starin'?" Joey motioned to the deck.

"I never win at this."

"I can tell," Joey grinned. "Pick a card. Call it."

"One ace, two queens," Miller smiled, figuring he had outwitted Joey by his dumb act.

"Read them and weep," Joey smiled, pulling in the cash on the bedspread as he laid down a royal flush.

"You . . ."

"What? Cheated? You sayin' I cheated? Look squirt. I don't have to cheat. For your information, new guy Private Miller from Kansas, I am known throughout Combat Command B of the First Armored Division as Corporal 'Lucky' Cipriano. You may call me Joey since we are in the same tank. But I am *lucky* for three reasons. Know what they are?"

"Okay, *lucky*. You tell me."

"Number one. Luck is opportunity disguised as hard work." He held up one finger. "Number two. Luck is timing," he said holding up another finger. "And, smart mouth, number three is that joker lying asleep right there."

"Sergeant O'Banyon? You call him lucky?"

Joey had Miller by the throat and began to squeeze. "We got to work together so I'm gonna make myself clear. He saved your sorry can at Gafsa, but you are too stupid to know it. Then he pulled off that stunning bit of miracle work where we knocked out four, count 'em, dip stick, that's four Tiger tanks at El Guettar with Patton himself watching—makes you, me, and Olsen look like genuises—he saved our first sergeant's life at Kasserine Pass, and he pulled me out of more questionable places than I care to count. He is the reason I'm here! He is the only man in this outfit I trust. You know why?" Joey let go of the stunned new tank gunner.

"Why?" Miller finally said as he cleared his throat. "You didn't have to do that."

"I want your full attention, bird brain. Here's why. You can trust Sergeant O'Banyon with your life, your wife, your kid, your dog . . . He keeps his word. Bein' with this guy is like riding with a priest. . . . He don't swear, don't drink. . . . He's honorable, that's why he's lucky. Besides. . . ." Joey took Miller's cards and shuffled them with his, ". . . from the first crap game when we got drafted until today, I always win when I hang around with him. You wanna play more, shoot dice maybe?"

"I fold," Miller said as he ambled back to his hospital cot.

"Just remember what I said about being lucky. Maybe some of it will wear off on ya."

"Joey," came the tired voice from the bed next to his. "That was real nice what you said about me," Peter smiled, awakening.

"You wasn't supposed to hear that. But since you did, I want you to do something for me," Joey said, pulling an ammo box out from under his bed. "I store this stuff behind my seat. If I die, it dies . . . but if for some reason it survives me, will you promise to get it to my parents in Jersey?" Joey watched for Peter's reply with a pleading demeanor. "It's all I've won since our first landing here in North Africa. I keep meanin' to send it home. You do that for me?"

Peter lay there noticing the green .30-caliber ammunition box with his name and serial number on it and smirked. "So, why did you put my name on it?"

" 'Cause everybody respects you. Nobody will cross you. That would be like stealing from the church. Me, on the other hand . . ." he laughed and shook his hand and head at the same moment. "And if they did steal from you, they know they'd have me and the family here to mess with." He smiled, patting his holstered .45 that was sitting on his cot with his other gear.

"You headed out?" Peter asked.

"Yeah. They guess my concussion ain't so bad, and I got half my hearing back. They're gonna put me in a supply outfit now that it looks like we are taking Bizerte and Tunis. In a truck, can you believe it?"

"The First Armored took Bizerte? Then its over. The Germans are finished."

"Not quite, but close. The brass think a couple weeks at best before the Germans surrender unconditionally. Their backs are to the sea, and our Navy is out there. Yeah, man. For all intents and purposes it's over. Can you believe it? They are actually giving *lucky* Cipriano a truck." He laughed at the irony. "Just what Patton told me I wasn't supposed to be driving."

Grinning from ear to ear, he whispered, "Can you imagine how much stuff I can haul in one of them six-cylinder duce-and-a-halfs? I can see my shingle out on the docks, *'Joey's Slightly Used War Souvenirs.'* "They both laughed hard at the remark.

"Slightly used," Peter still laughed. "Yeah, somehow I can see it," he posed, wiping the tears away caused by the image of Joey at work making a buck off of the incongruity in terms.

"I'm gonna be pickin' up surrendering Gerries. They're walkin' in from all over Tunisia, hundreds of thousands of 'em with 9-milimeter pistols, bayonets, medals. . . . The Navy guys back in Oran buy this stuff. . . . One guy paid me $100 for that Nazi flag I picked off that burnt out Gerry tank at Sidi-bou-Zid, the day before Kasserine.

"Now the Navy will be coming right into Bizerte and Tunis. And my truck? Guess where it will be loaded with relics of war?"

"You are one helluva *lucky* guy, Joey."

"Hey, when you start talkin' like that?"

"Like what?"

"Swearin'."

"*Helluva* you mean?" Peter laughed. "*Hell* doesn't seem like such a bad word to me anymore. Not after what we've seen."

They both silently nodded and paused to digest the thought.

"Well, anyway, swearin' don't fit you. Leave that to me, okay, Pete?"

"Yeah, sure. Guess I won't be much help to you. They won't split us up, will they?"

"Naw. I know this captain in supply, see. I got it all worked out. He's gettin' a cut as long as the orders come through for you to drive with me. You are a walking-wounded, they say. Walking, riding, what's the difference?"

"Really. Who said?"

"The doctor. Heard him say the leg gash is healin' fine. They thought you might've fractured it, too, but the x-rays showed nothin' more than a bad bruise."

"Yeah, those Gerry 88's can bruise a man real bad. How about Olsen and Miller?"

Miller heard him and waved. "Fine, Sarge. Thanks for hauling me the hell out of there."

"Think nothing of it," Pete waved. "How about Olsen?"

Joey tilted his head in the sleeping man's direction.

"Damn." Peter shook his head. "Man, all I remember is running like crazy to get away from that tank, Olsen on my heels, and you and Miller ahead of us. What they saying about him?"

"He caught some shrapnel when we were on that dead run after our tank got hit. He'll be okay. Less one leg. But alive is better than the alternative. Ya know, bein' lead tank and all, I wonder if General Patton saw it. Maybe he was watchin' with those granddaddy binoculars of his. I've been thinkin', ya know him telling me not to lose another tank? Maybe he saw it and knows it wasn't my fault." Joey laughed morosely at his own comment and then waxed serious.

"Maybe he saw me scrambling like hell, driving that thing through all of those explosions trying to save us. He sure as hell didn't see me throw it in reverse, did he?"

"No, he didn't, Joey."

"Maybe he saw Johnson's tank blown to hell. Maybe Patterson's, too."

Peter thought he detected sudden emotion in Joey's voice as he witnessed the usually stoic Italian clench his teeth hard.

"Yeah. Maybe."

"They were fine fellas . . . all of 'em. I can't get over how we can be laughin' one minute and dead the next." Joey shook his head.

Peter reached out his hand as Joey gathered up his gear. "You promise to come and get me out of here. Maybe tomorrow, the next day? We can be business partners in this new enterprise?" Peter smiled.

"You don't worry about nothin'," Joey smiled back as he took Peter's hand. "You're my lucky charm. Big brother is lookin' out for us. Well, I hear some Italian prisoners are bein' picked up today. Think I'll go talk some of those lousy Nazi-lovin' traitor cousins of mine out of some of their hard-earned, Mussolini-made *lire.*"

"Take care, Joey. I'll be watching for you."

Their customary parting and greeting signal shared—

thumbs up—Joey stopped at the hospital-tent door with gear in tow. "You'll always be my lucky charm," Joey smiled.

Peter lay back in his cot then reached for a book he had seldom taken time with during his five months in North Africa. Almost every page had some writing on it.

It was the *Five Year Diary* Anna asked him to keep. *Five years!* he thought. It was too much to try to contemplate that this war could last for five years.

He didn't have the stomach to tell the whole truth. To talk about starving kids; bombed-out tanks with enemy and American dead fried to almost nothing more than a shadow on the ground; body parts scattered over the battle field; wounded crying for mom and home, scared out of their wits every time the sound of planes was heard in the distance; days, weeks without bathing; constant diarrhea, cold, heat, dust, smoke, explosions.

The glory of war! Who in the hell thought that line up? he asked himself. Whoever it was either had never really been to war or was sick, crazy out of his mind, a distorted excuse for a real man.

But his having written a few lines each day, or every other day at least, meant this wasn't just a dream, a nightmarish journey into the nether land of things only concocted in the most twisted of minds.

This was war, and it was hell, and he would never have to go to hell, he guessed, having been there once. Maybe his kids would read his diary and realize what he and the men he fought with were doing here in their youth. Maybe there was some value in it.

He was too far away from life, the lighthouse, and the only thing that mattered to him. He read a couple of pages.

Why even try to keep a journal? he thought to himself. His mind went back to Uncle Billie at the lighthouse. Each night he wrote in that old logbook of his. *For what?* He had often asked himself as a boy. *What's the old man doing? Writing about how many seagulls flew over Port Hope today?*

He never had asked Uncle Billie. But it was uncharacteristic of Uncle Billie to spend time on something that didn't matter.

So what was he to write about this damnable war? The countless hours of sheer boredom punctuated by moments of absolute terror? He'd already written about Joey and a few other soldiers. He even described what a light M3 Sherman was in comparison to a Sherman M4 tank: the armor thickness; the 75-milimeter shell and its velocity; how many 7.52-millimeter machine guns, the .30 calibers, and one .50 caliber versus the Panzer Tigers, Mark III's, Mark IV's that they were up against.

He'd already described the countryside. Now he was down to events. Just the events of the day. Someday he'd have to read that lighthouse logbook and get an idea of what a man wrote about on an island where nothing happened.

Peter read a few of the passages scribbled in the diary:

Feb. 14, 1943

Things going good. A couple of enemy planes strafed us. One shot down. Heading off to attack. English have Germans pushed our way. No hot food for a week.

Feb. 19, 1943

Tank hit. Myers dead. Clamser serious condition. Drove three days and three nights in full retreat from a place called Kasserine Pass. Never been so scared or tired in my entire life. Can't believe what I saw. Can't believe I'm still alive.

Feb. 20, 1943

Clamser alive. I was almost arrested. Was going to kill a doctor unless he treated him. Didn't know the gun was unloaded. What's happening to me? Joey came to the rescue.

Feb. 28, 1943

Clamser shipped home. Don't know if he'll make it. We're sitting around dug in somewhere out in the desert. Cold and rainy. Gerries bomb us every day. Joey and me are digging the deepest hole ever dug by man. Won't this damn rain ever stop? An officer tried to recruit me for a patrol. Told him where to go. First time I've ever done that.

March 8, 1943

Back in Algeria with new tank. New crew members, Olsen, radioman, and gunner. Miller loader. New Sherman M4 medium tank. It's about time. Was given medal today by General Patton. Joey told me off for volunteering to be lead tank in next battle. I didn't volunteer. Joey got the bronze. I got the silver and made sergeant. I'm not trying to be a hero. Just want to go home. Got a letter from my sweetheart today.

31

I'LL BE okay, Anna. Don't ya worry. I've got Hal here at the docks and Laddie, my mutt, ta keep me company at the lighthouse." Billie helped Anna up the steps to the small ferryboat that Hal operated on its daily run to Nantucket Island for supplies and mail.

"I'll be back as soon as the baby is old enough to make the trip," Anna responded warmly with a gentle hug around the neck and a kiss on the whiskered cheeks of the old lighthouse keeper.

"Laddie and me will be watchin' for ya. Write me now. And tell Peter not ta forget me," he waved as the boat pulled away from the dock.

"Well, Laddie, there she goes. The brightest light we had out here. Oh, how I'll miss her. Well, we'd better get on back."

Billie walked the two miles back up the hill from the boat docks. He wasn't concerned about his heart but was more concerned with living sickly, so he did what he could to act like the healthy man he had always been.

"A man's heart isn't necessarily broken by what he eats and drinks, is it, Laddie?" the old man huffed as he neared the top of the hill. He looked out over the ocean home he had known for twenty-odd years. He had come here to get away and live out his days alone.

How could he know his brother's boy would change all that? How could he know this young woman would take him back and make him feel so young and alive, so much full of love for Katie who had been gone all these years?

"I've got ta write to my boy over there in North Africa, Laddie. This one thing has been on my mind, and I'd better do it now."

He patted the sheepdog's matted head. "Then a bath fer you, fella," he said, reaching up to his chest. The pain shot down his arm and then went away. "Ah, Katie, come back ta me, won't ya?" he whispered as he gazed out to sea.

Anna was concerned. "Hal?" she asked over the drone and clank of the antiquated fishing-ship's engine.

"Yes, dear?" Hal responded, eyes still ahead while he pointed the old but sturdy vessel out from the island to open sea, some fifteen miles from Nantucket.

"Uncle Billie didn't look so good this morning. I'm feeling guilty leaving him like that."

"What about you?" he motioned to her large extra weight at her middle. "You've got two people to worry about right there, and Billie knows it."

"I know, but it doesn't make me feel any better," she sighed, holding her tummy with both hands.

Hal was silent as he thought about her feelings. There wasn't anything to say really. "Heard from Peter?" he finally asked.

Hal delivered the island's mail to its fifty-odd inhabitants and, of course, he knew she had heard from Peter. He just wanted her to think about something else and to take her mind off worrying about things she couldn't control.

"He's fine now. His arm wound has healed, he says. He's driving for a transportation battalion, taking prisoners from one camp to the next. I guess with the fighting being over in North Africa, it will be awhile before he gets back into a tank. Whenever that is, its too soon for me," she shuddered.

"Like to steer this old tub?" Hal smiled, changing the topic.

"Really? You trust me?"

"Nothin' to it. Just maintain the course set on that compass heading right there. See the needle?"

"Yes, I see it. Okay," she smiled.

"That a girl. If Peter could see you now, he'd be mightily proud of how ya took care of his uncle."

"Really?" she looked back at him.

"Really," he smiled.

32

THE MEN eagerly surrounded the sergeant handing out mail, snatching at it like starving refugees for a morsel of food. Peter grabbed his letter and found his way to the tailgate of the supply truck he had been assigned to drive.

My darling Peter,

You will be happy to know our little girl has your eyes, my nose, your mouth, my hair, and the cutest dimples when she smiles. We had agreed to naming her Kathleen in honor of Uncle Billie's wife. She fits the name so well. I don't think we should call her Katie, though. I like her proper name, Kathleen. Isn't it a sweet-sounding name?

I hold her, rock her, feed her, and almost can't believe I'm a mother at nineteen years old. I'm so happy to have her finally here. Enclosed is a black and white of her being held by the nurse in our ward, Sally Murphy, who helped bring her into the world.

I feel fine. I didn't experience all the labor I thought I would. Kathleen just sort of "arrived" on schedule.

I have written to Uncle Billie to share the news with him. I hope to be with him in one month, as soon as Kathleen is old enough to travel. Mother doesn't care for the idea, as I will be leaving ahead of them, but then they will be coming for the summer tourist season anyway to run the general store, as always, in late June.

We are all so grateful to know you are not in one of those Sherman tanks anymore. I sleep much better knowing you are safe behind the wheel of a supply truck. We pray that somehow Hitler will just give up and the Japanese, too, and then this awful war will end. Too many of our boys from here in Connecticut won't ever come home.

I haven't heard any news about your old sailing buddies, Chad and Tom, from Nantucket. They're both in the Pacific now and the Marines are taking Island after Island. I pray for them, too. I will let you know if I hear from their parents. I dropped them a card asking for their sons' addresses.

Well, its feeding time again. Our baby is gorgeous and healthy. You will be so proud. I love you, darling. I pray for you always.

> *Your devoted wife,*
> *Anna*

"Hey, Pete, what's the wife say?" Joey asked, chomping down on a half-smoked stogie.

"Oh, nothing much," Peter grinned, tucking the letter safely in his pocket. "I'm a father!" he screamed, jumping off the tailgate of the supply truck they both occupied. He ran up to the cab and pulled out a box of cigars he had purchased in New York and started throwing them all around the bivouac area.

"I'm a dad! It's a girl!" he shouted with uncharacteristic exuberance. "Miller, here you go," he said, throwing two cigars to the former tank-crew member assigned supply duty with him and Joey.

"Joey, this one is for you. It's special. Cuban. I saved it for this occasion. Will you be my girl's godfather?"

"Me? You want me to be a godfather? Wait until the family in Jersey gets a load of this. Of course. Sure I'll be. . . . What's her name?"

"Kathleen. Her name is Kathleen," Peter shouted so everyone could hear.

"Joey Cipriano, godfather. I like the ring to that," he laughed, congratulating his buoyant Irish pal. "Now, when we get to Italy, I'll make 'em all bow with respect and call me *Padrino.*"

"Hey, you fellas hear the news?" a transportation sergeant called out as he pulled up in a jeep. "It's officially over!"

"The war? Hey, you guys hear that? The war's over! We're goin' home!" Joey shouted to the crowd of soldiers lounging around, reading letters, and lighting up.

The sergeant tried to calm them down but to no avail. Booze started to be passed around, horns were honked, and soldiers started dancing wildly in response to the news.

"It's over here in North Africa, you dopes. . . . North Africa . . . not the war," the sergeant shouted until he finally got some of their attention.

"Hey, Mac, you sure you heard right?" Joey asked. "Maybe

it is all over. Maybe you just heard wrong. Maybe the Nazi's quit fighting here in Tunisia because its all over . . . *kaput,* *finis,* the end . . . for Hitler and his goose-stepping pals."

"No way, Cipriano. In your dreams. It's only over here in Tunisia. Von Arnim, the Kraut general who took over for Rommel, surrendered his final hold-out divisions south of here today."

"Well, I'm drinkin' anyway," Joey said, taking a long swig of French bourbon. "I've been savin' this, but I can get more. To the end of the war!" he shouted and passed the bottle around while the other soldiers went back to reading and letterwriting.

"So what do you think is next?" Pete asked his drinking godfather friend.

"Sicily, Italy, France . . . they got to be liberated before we get to Berlin. My bet is we get our tank back in one of those places in a couple of months. Man, I'll miss this truck and all this dough I've been makin'. I got twenty 'G's' already stashed in the bank back home," he said, taking a long gulp from the rest of the bottle's contents.

"Twenty 'G's' as in 20,000 dollars?" Peter asked, mouth agape.

"Shhh," Joey motioned with a finger over his lips. "Yeah, that's right. What do you think I've been doing all this time, just barely getting by? Buying War Bonds maybe?"

"Man, Joey, that's a lot of money," Peter stammered in amazement. "I got maybe 1,000 dollars saved up. War Bonds."

"Look, little brother. You got to quit bein' so conservative. Ya got to get out with me at night. Get in the business with me. Quit holdin' back. I'll cut ya in. Ya just got to get the 'big picture' about war and its spoils," Joey said, using his hands as if painting a scene for Peter.

"See, war is all about killin' people and destroyin' things, right?"

"I guess so," Peter replied, dumb struck at such an accurate and simple definition coming from Joey's mouth.

"Well, while them generals are getting all their glory, movin' up higher and higher by havin' us poor slobs go out and butcher each other and wreak havoc on towns and the countryside, I figure they aren't gonna get Joey Cipriano so cheap. . . . What, 50 dollars per month?"

"Yeah, we work cheap, don't we?" Peter nodded wryly.

"You're damn right," Joey emphasized with a finger to his friend's chest. "So I'm gamblin' 'cause it's fun. And I'm a 'collector' of war artifacts," he laughed, " 'cause it's fun, too. So I make a real livin' while I'm doin' their dirty work. Right?" He nudged Peter who was sitting next to him. "Right?"

"So, what if you get caught? See, that's what I got a problem with. If we both start doing this, who's going to bail us out of trouble? I mean, I'm always able to get your can out of the fire, right?" Peter responded.

"Well, that is a consideration. Guess I should make you a silent partner," he said, slapping Peter on the back and lighting up the stogie hanging from his lips.

"I'm pleased as pie to just be Pete, the lucky charm," Peter said as he jumped off the tailgate of the supply truck. "You just drive good when we get to wherever we're headed, like you have been, and I'll be plenty happy. The best thing you can do for me is help get me home alive."

"You got it partner," Joey winked and snapped his fingers. "Where you headed?"

"Bizerte. See that jeep over there? I'm headed to find out all I can about what's up."

"Hold on, amigo. I'm comin' with ya."

．．．

Billie was more tired than he had been since Anna had left months earlier. He took each step slowly, deliberately, as he climbed the lighthouse steps to light the lamp for the night.

He didn't have to do this, he knew. He could give it all up. But he'd made himself a promise to keep lighting the lamp, at least until Peter returned, and to keep his promise made years ago, to watch for his Katie.

It was a token, really. A gesture. A gesture of love to be sure but of faith, also. He was a lightkeeper, a solitary job dedicated to give power to others to see when they needed it most. He'd rather die than give up on that. A lonely cause, it was, but a good one.

He stopped half-way up the stairs, out of breath. He waited and then hummed the song he first whistled when he met Kathleen all those years ago in Central Park. "The Rose of Tralee" it was. *And what a rose she was*, he thought.

He continued up the steps until he finally reached the lamp. He had turned down the Lighthouse Commission's request to automate the lamp with electricity. He liked the old ways, the parabolic oil lantern. It was familiar and made him feel more useful than merely throwing a switch could.

He had secretly purchased the lighthouse, too. No one knew that. The lighthouse had fulfilled its purpose years ago, since the early days of radio and, now, radar navigation. Except for the civil-defense hat he also wore, the old lighthouse was a silent sentinel in the dark night, standing alone beyond the Northeast shores to signal to all ships and newcomers to America that there was hope, that some things never changed, that some things stayed and remained sure.

He had already had his Last Will and Testament drafted to ensure that the lighthouse would remain in the family until

Peter lived out his life. Then it would become a property for the park service to use as it saw fit.

He was happy with that agreement. Peter and his Anna and all their beloved little ones would have a home for many decades to come, if that is what they chose. He would be remembered, and the legacy would live on.

He ambled around the light, polishing the brass as he went. His left side ached and a burning sensation ran down his arm, but he couldn't be bothered with that.

Anna had written, and she was coming the next week with the baby. "Kathleen," he smiled as he polished and whistled the Irish tune, forgetting about the pain.

Billie poured oil into the lamp and secured the shiny brass cap tightly. The lighthouse was spotless, ready for any inspection it might be given. He was pleased with his work. He lit the light and slowly headed, step by careful step, down to the main floor. He wanted to make sure everything was ready.

Anna wouldn't be here for a week, but you never know, he told himself. *She could come early.* He found the logbook and sat and made his entry. Laddie was at his feet. He wrote:

The lamp is lit on this May 13, 1943. I will take a rest now. My darlin' Anna and her wee one, Kathleen, is comin' soon. Peter wrote me last week, and I cherish his sweet words of love. The good Lord has protected him so far, and I'm sure will bring him safely home from this terrible conflict.

I have sealed a letter to Peter, and I place it here in the logbook on this page. It will move from page to page till the lad comes home. I hope to deliver it to him myself, but if not, then the Lord's will be done.

"Come with me, Laddie. Don't ya think the night is fair? Look how the light shines out ta sea. Look, Laddie. See the pier. It's as if the twirling light reflects the dancing of my darlin's. . . . The way it used ta be.

"If I weren't in my right mind, I'd swear. . . ." he said aloud and hurried from the door, stumbling across the meadow to the hill overlooking the bay.

"I'd swear," he said, hurrying as he gripped his chest, racing toward the light.

Laddie whimpered as he followed close behind his master's steps to the edge of the hill. Something unfamiliar was calling to his master. Protectively, he stayed close at Billie's side as the old man gazed anxiously out to sea.

"I could have sworn, Laddie. I could have sworn I saw her fair figure, wavin' to me, calling my name. Oh . . ." he groaned, cupping both hands to his chest and falling to his knees.

"Dear God in heaven," he pled, kneeling, head bowed, into the grassy earth beneath him.

He strained to raise his eyes once more to search out beyond his island home to the sea, face flushed with pain as he gasped for breath. "Dear God. Can it be?" he panted, desperately, begging for clearness of sight through moisture heavy eyes.

"Katie?" his puzzled expression suddenly posed. A smile now erased the contorted expressions of pain on his face, and dried, his watering eyes.

With great effort he raised himself up as Laddie whimpered. Billie's arms were outstretched, seeming to draw in the image which enveloped him. "Katie . . ." he whispered.

33

ANNA TEARFULLY rummaged throughout the lighthouse, looking for traces of where her beloved Uncle Billie might have last been. It had been four days since the funeral, and the fresh grave out back reminded her of the love affair he had here. Nothing could separate him from this place but death itself.

Maybe he was finally at peace. Maybe Katie came to him like he dreamed, she thought to herself. She hoped he hadn't suffered. Hal had found him out on the edge of the hill, collapsed as if he had been there to take a final look at the bay. No one would ever be sure what happened.

Anna had been amazed at the crowd that had gathered from far and near for the simple service. A former sea captain friend of Billie's, who had been asked years before by Billie during the first war, officiated at his grave.

A religious man and Protestant deacon, Captain Hall had agreed, sure that he would never live long enough to keep his promise to Billie. But at seventy years old he had outlived him. For his Catholic friend Billie, he offered a simple but ponderous eulogy and benediction, adding the traditional Catholic blessings of the grave as a gesture to Billie's Irish faith.

Anna dusted off the old leather-bound logbook with a quick puff of air from her lips and picked it up. It fell open to the final entry Uncle Billie had made, and she finally understood as she read it.

"You dear, sweet old man," she smiled as she read his lonely final words written on May 13, 1943.

She picked up the sealed envelope from the pages of the logbook where it sat marking the final entry and started to open it, but she wondered if she hadn't better respect Uncle Billie's wish to let her husband, Peter, have his moment alone with Uncle Billie, reading his letter at the grave when he returned from the war.

She placed the letter back in the pages and closed the book, placing it where it always had been, on the nightstand next to the comfortable padded rocker where she would spend so much time waiting for Peter to return from the war.

Their baby daughter, Kathleen, was asleep in the cradle that Uncle Billie must have made. It was the first thing she saw when she opened the door to the musty lighthouse. A simple note was attached to the cradle: *For my darling Kathleen. From your loving Uncle Billie.*

Should she tell Peter? She wondered what Uncle Billie would want. In the hospital at the time of his last recovery, he had asked her not to tell Peter, not to concern him. But this was different. He was dead.

She gazed at her surroundings, her new home. She had read the will, given her by the attorney in charge of Uncle Billie's sizable estate. She was astounded at his wealth, the savings which he had amassed. A record of the deed to the

Dabney estate in Ireland and the records of all the village folk of Kilgore whose debts he had cleared were before her to marvel at.

She wondered if Peter knew. She doubted it. Billie had been so unassuming, so quiet about any affairs outside of his simple work at Port Hope Island.

He had left a sizable amount in an annuity for three different charities in New York: a children's health and medical fund at St. Joseph's Hospital, monthly funds for an orphanage, and an aid fund set aside specifically for indigent immigrants from Ireland.

He had invested everything he had ever earned in bonds, stocks, treasury bills, and he owned the lighthouse, paid free and clear. Those earnings now funded the charities well, and an amount Anna had never imagined possible was set aside for Peter, herself, and their children for the maintenance of the lighthouse and for their children's education.

It was theirs now for a generation to come. She would rather have Uncle Billie forever, though. Whatever he was before he met his beloved Katie, however rough he had assured her he had been, something wonderful happened during their brief time together and after. *How had he become such a man as this?*

Anna wondered if she could ever be for Peter what Katie had been for Billie.

Peter sat on the beach outside Bizerte rereading the letter from home. Joey wanted to spend some time at a bar on the main road, but Peter just wanted to be alone with his thoughts. So he came out here. The roads were cleared from mines, the drive pleasant, the sky clear and blue, the breeze off the Mediterranean Sea soothing.

The Arabs, native Tunisians, all waved like he was a conquering hero as he drove by. Young French Tunisian girls blew kisses.

He wondered how Uncle Billie was making out alone there on the island. The heart attack had worried him. He had no one in the world but Anna and now his infant daughter. He wouldn't get to know her for only God knew how long.

It seemed to take weeks to get letters back and forth. He wished he could talk to Billie now, here on the shore. He wished he could ask him questions on how to live, how to be, what to do now, during the war, after the war.

"Uncle Billie, do you believe in God?" he had asked him once.

"Aye, lad. Don't ya know I believe?" he had responded.

"I guess so. It's just we don't go to church."

"A bit hard way out here, but yer right. We should go." Then he added. "Bein' religious doesn't mean yer a spiritual man, Peter, any more than bein' spiritual means yer a religious man."

Peter wondered at that statement for a long time. He learned that in combat, even the biggest sinner, the loudest swearing atheist, is religious in a foxhole. When artillery or an enemy plane had them zeroed in, men who never prayed recited "Hail Mary's" like they were in a race against a stop watch to see how many they could say in record time.

From the first day Peter had questioned his uncle on the subject, they went every Sunday, during good weather or bad, to Nantucket Island to visit the churches of different faiths, Uncle Billie being a respecter of them all.

"Why don't we just stick with one?" he remembered asking his Irish Catholic uncle.

"Oh, when I find the right one, maybe I will. I look for God everywhere," he said simply and that was that.

Peter knew of his uncle's deep devotion. He found him once upon his knees deep in prayer, saying simple things, like he was thinking out loud. Ever since then Peter prayed like that.

He thought about the man who never swore and didn't drink, except upon special celebrations. An Irishman who didn't drink was like blaspheming against the saints. He knew plenty of Irishmen and to a man they swore like bandits and drank like horses.

Uncle Billie wouldn't recognize him now, almost one year since he had left for the induction center, a young boy married to Anna. It seemed a lifetime ago.

He wasn't a boy anymore, but wasn't sure he was a man, either. He just didn't like the feeling he had about the killing. He had, along with his tank crew, done their jobs. They shot first or shot better, and God knew they had lost their own tanks twice and that plenty of the men he came over with from the States were buried in the graveyards in Algeria and here in Tunisia.

Clamser had died in the States from some infection. His wife had written to Peter offering thanks for saving his life. *Saving it for what?*

Other GI's were in the surf playing. *Killing like men yesterday, playing like kids today,* he realized and shook his head. He closed his eyes, laid back on the sand, and shut out their happy noisemaking as he listened to the pounding surf of the Mediterranean Sea upon the white sandy Tunisian beach.

The heat felt good on his face. The salty air took him back. The waves noisily chased the sandpipers up and down the shore as they crashed upon the sand . . . taking him back. He could go home any time he wanted to if he could hear the ocean speak to him this way every day.

34

PORT HOPE ISLAND
PRESENT DAY

THE NIGHT'S cloak had worn thin as evidenced by the rising sun on the eastern horizon. Peter had dozed off just moments earlier as he finished the oral history for his daughter, Kathleen, who sleepily sat vigil, watching the tired lighthouse keeper relieve the burden of memory from himself. Dozing off from time to time, wrapped in blanket on the sofa, she reminded herself of the urgency her father felt for this telling of his life history.

With dawn, his sleepless eyes ceased to behold the vision of his youth before him. Kathleen was now fully awakened to the new day by the sound of the foghorn from the docks two miles away.

"Oh, Dad," she yawned, brushing away the sleep that had momentarily caught her off guard. "Are you alright?" she asked as she sat up and threw the light coverlet off her.

"I'm fine. A little thirsty," he answered with a hoarse sound to his voice.

"Here," she offered, coming back from the kitchen with a glass of water and the straw to sip from. He drained the glass. Kathleen spent the morning hours changing him, bathing him, and feeding a liquid breakfast to her skeletal-looking father, all to ready him for his final Sunday at the lighthouse before returning to Kathleen's home.

"The fog is lifting. That is good," her father announced matter-of-factly as he sat at the open door of the cottage with a blanket covering his legs. "Sundays always were my favorite days, you know," he smiled, looking back over his shoulder at Kathleen who struggled for composure at the kitchen sink. "A day of rest, you know," he added.

"I know," she replied in a barely audible voice.

"Well, I'm ready. Would you like to sit with me this afternoon on the hill? I'd enjoy it if you spent sunset with me," he added in a weak, strained tone of voice.

Why was every word he uttered so potently weighed with ominousness? she wondered. *"Day of rest, sunset" . . . as if he were carefully considering each word,* she thought.

"I'd like that, too. I'll bring my canvas and finish that painting of the pier and cove while we talk," she said, wiping her hands dry. "You don't seem as tired as you should be after such a long night," she added.

"That would be grand," he replied, miles away in thought, apparently not hearing all she said.

A feeling of serene repose filled his ravaged body. He wondered where the strength was coming from. Life had passed as if it were all a dream. Now, he felt no pain.

"You should take a nap before we go out, don't you think?"

He looked up to his daughter who stood over him, gripping

the handles to his wheelchair. He just smiled. She knew what his eyes were telling her.

"You stubborn man," she whispered as she kissed his cheek and began to push him toward the place where meadow and seashore met, the edge of the slope that tumbled to the surf below.

Kathleen fixed the brakes on the wheelchair and stood for a moment in silence.

Peter absorbed the refreshing sea breeze and drank in the sight of his beloved ocean. Kathleen breathed deeply, too, as if she could save this moment forever by doing so.

"I'll be right back, Dad. I'm going to get the canvas and paints. I need my chair, too," she said as she left him to his pondering. *How fitting*, she thought.

Like the serene seascapes of paintings adorning the walls of homes and art galleries across America, she had actually lived with an old man of the sea, at a lighthouse, on a windswept island. Unbeknownst to Peter, he was the embodiment of the romantic notions a thousand artists had tried to capture with their tinctures and brushes.

Peter gazed upon the scene wondering why he never tired of it. How *lucky* he had been! Ah, but for the fires of his life, if it had not been for them, maybe he would be holding Anna's hand now in this twilight hour. He could have had the perfect life here on Port Hope if not for those fires that smouldered in his mind.

Lucky. "Joey," he smiled. He wondered about Joey and where his own youth had gone when it was destroyed by war. But he smiled. He had always done his best. Maybe it wasn't good enough, but it was *his* best.

"Kathleen, darling?" he posed as she returned and began to set up her painting easel and watercolors.

"Yes, Dad?"

"I want to finish my story."

"I thought you might."

"It was a long road home to Port Hope from the war . . . and to today," he reminisced.

She reached into her handbag and sat the lighthouse logbook on his lap. "Thought you might want this," she added. She wasn't sure why he cared so much about it but knew it was important to him. She set the canvas up. "I've almost got it now, Dad. The pier is looking good, but I'm not sure how to finish it."

"I'm sure," he breathed, inaudible to Kathleen.

"What's that, Dad?"

"I'll show you how to finish the canvas when I finish my story," he breathed heavily.

Tranquil but heavy, he thought to himself of his body. "Oh, Kathleen. Yes. It's here with me now. Everything is here and very clear," he said.

"Okay," she said simply as she picked up her brush to begin stroking the final scene on the canvas. She couldn't be sure what he was thinking, but she still had him with her and would keep him as long as she could, if listening made the difference.

She wasn't anxious to finish the painting, either. She held out the vain childlike hope that the painting, unfinished, meant he wouldn't really leave her. She brushed lightly upon the canvas.

He began to speak as if his storytelling were for a larger audience.

35

A T FIRST, the landing at Anzio was easy. We caught the Germans napping, literally. Two hundred Germans defended this coastal town at the base of the Alban mountain range. We went in there on January 16, 1944, swinging around the German western flank and coming in behind them from the sea.

"Although we had been in Italy since September, down around Salerno Bay, we had been slugging it out with the Germans lately in an attempt to drive them off the Italian peninsula with the aid of our British allies. They made a stubborn resistence and held at a place called Monte Cassino and the Rapido River.

"Going around them seemed like a good idea. Besides, if we captured Anzio and made it a new beachhead, there would be nothing stopping us from taking Rome and cutting off the German retreat from the south. Rome was but a day's jeep ride up Highway 7 from Anzio. So the Generals, Eisenhower,

Alexander, and Prime Minister Winston Churchill sent us in with General Lucas' Sixth Army Corps.

"Our big mistake was taking nine days to establish a beachhead, allowing the Germans to ring the hills around us with their big guns, the 88 millimeters. It would become a four-month killing ground with the enemy holding the high ground while we dodged artillery fire, probing their front lines with our tanks and infantry and trying to make a soggy breakout in one of the wettest winters on record for the region.

"There were days when we could do nothing but make our hole-in-the-ground homes deeper and deeper. We had to dig our tanks in and use them like artillery because the constant rain stopped them from getting anywhere near the front lines. Rumor had it that the tanks were being reserved for the real punch out of the beachhead.

"But too many enemy direct hits had obliterated whole tank crews because there was no "behind the lines" at Anzio, not even for our supply-company buddies who had taken us in during the months we recovered from our wounds after the Tunisia campaign. We were getting angrier all the time at sitting like ducks in a shooting gallery, and mad about losing our friends in these artillery duels. We were anxious for action but were told to stay put.

"Joey, he was really something. Amid all this horror of being shelled every day, strafed, bombed, and living in muddy hell, he seemed in his element. Crap games, poker, dice, betting on the number of hours between shellings—you name it, he had a real business going. As long as I was there, he sure enough remained lucky.

"The few times I was on guard duty or ran into Naples for something on orders from the company commander, he'd lose his shirt. He would never bet, gamble, or wager unless I was present. It was an odd partnership, really. An Italian and Irish Catholic together. One was irreverent, loving being in Italy, doing deals with the locals, running into town every chance he got for . . . as he would say, attending confession a lot; and then there was me, thinking all the time about one thing, home. I wasn't willing to anger God either by giving in to all the temptations that surrounded army life. I wanted to make sure I was on God's side, just in case I really needed him, and just in case I didn't make it home.

"It was in late February that Joey had worked some deal with the supply battalion to work on a truck that went back and forth between Naples harbor to the south and back to Anzio, about a sixty mile trip. He was setting himself up real good."

Peter's voice relaxed while his daughter continued painting. "Dad? Everything alright?"

"Hum? Oh, yes, sweetheart. Just thinking about a Sunday in Italy. It was a bright, pleasant day, like this. If it hadn't been for the war, the scene of that small Italian town, even though in rubble, and the ocean could be captivating, like this scene is today."

Kathleen let him wander back to that day. He seemed more energized now, and she was hopeful that God had many more weeks for him to be with her, somehow. *As long as the energy stays up, he'll be okay,* she assured herself.

"Look, Joey, I don't know. What if we suddenly get orders to move out. What do I tell Lieutenant Kirby?"

"We ain't moving out. Number one, there's the problem of mud. Number two, I got a direct line on all the scuttlebutt at Division HQ. See, I got this friend there; he owes me big time."

"I ought to be going with you, I guess, to keep you out of trouble."

"You don't need to worry about me, little brother," the Jersey Italian laughed. "I found religion," he grinned, gently cupping Peter's face in his hands with a wake-up slap.

"You what?"

"Yeah, you know. Boozin' and chasin' broads gets old Pete. You're lookin' at the new Joey, not that I'm gonna become a priest or nothin' like that."

Peter couldn't help snickering at the "new Joey."

"No, I'm dead serious. I mean maybe I'm not gonna give up a good glass of wine now and then, but I've decided it's time for a change. *Nuvo persona.* I got this idea, see. I see all these kids starving and stuff, and ya know I think to myself, *Self? You got all these great connections in supply, up at division HQ. The money is good from gambling, and what is the Army doing about these Italian brothers and sisters of mine?* My mother was born in Napoli, you know."

"No, I didn't know that."

"Yeah, I've got cousins and everything down there. Remember that one night we ate with Francesca, the girl with the . . ." he used hand gestures to describe her. "She fed us until we had to be picked up by an ambulance? Remember that?"

"Yeah," Peter laughed, shaking his head.

"Francesca Donatello Cipriano. Yeah, we're first cousins."

"Why didn't you tell me?" Peter spit out between cackles. Just listening to Joey talk was like sitting at the feet of a master storyteller, everything was exaggerated but was somehow believable if it was Joey spinning it.

"Because. Well, I wanted you to think I had this thing going with her, to keep up my reputation. You know Italian men are blessed with more . . . let's say intimate vigor than the Irish or other Anglos."

Miller, the radioman from the Midwest, chimed in from the far end of the underground dugout, "Says who?"

"So tell me, big mouth. What you got goin' lately?" Joey shot back.

No reply from Miller. Just a wave of the hand that said "get lost." He continued to read his dime-store novel.

"So here I am with all these connections, see. And the people are getting their houses bombed out by both sides in this lousy war. I'm not supposed to help out *la famiglia?*"

"You mean you're not making a profit?" Peter asked incredulously.

"No margin? Of course, there's a margin. How do I keep all these favors lined up around "Old Ironsides" if there's no margin. But I split it with the family in Napoli, and we take stuff to an orphanage. I make sure it gets directly to all the hungry, naked, starving kids first and then, who knows? After the war, maybe I'll come back to good old Napoli and start an import and export business to Jersey, New York."

"Man, this war is made for a guy like you," Peter laughed, slapping his big Italian friend on the back as he sat down on some sandbags to try to get control of his snickering.

"What's so funny?"

"You. You are the bright spot in this war, Joey. I love ya, man," he said, wiping at the moisture coming to his eyes from the comic relief Joey had given him.

"You mean that, Pete?" Joey said with a broad smile.

"Well, I just said it, didn't I?"

"Ya know, you'd make a good Italian. Very sensitive . . ."

Joey responded. "I've been watchin' you, Pete. You really got your act straight."

"Just following orders from an old lighthouse keeper," he grinned, leaning back against the sandbag wall of the dugout, six feet underground.

"That's what I like about you. You are pure. I never knew nobody like that before. You come from some island without dames and booze and here you are standin' before me . . . a bright shinin' example of what maybe I can become."

Peter flushed red with embarrassment. "I'm not perfect, just stupid, maybe."

"No, you're perfect man. I swear, Pete, you are," Joey replied with unusual and affectionate candor. "No bull. Everybody knows we're lucky cause you got God on your side."

Peter just shook his head.

"See, I got this one sideline thing going on I haven't told nobody about. There's this pretty Italian dame in Naples, see, and her parents, they like me, but her mama gave me a tongue lashin' I ain't gonna forget for bringin' her home late on one of my "supply trips" last month. Then Loretta, that's the chick's name, she said she was a different kind of girl, a good girl . . . You get the drift. Well, then she says to me she wants to get married but in the church wearin' white, see, and she says she'll only marry a man of honor. So, bein' crazy about this dame, I start thinkin' maybe if I'm a bit more like Pete, I'll get the *honor* she and the *famiglia* thinks I got. At least I told them I got honor."

"Gee, Joey. Congratulations! That's swell!" Peter said, raising himself up to shake Joey's hand. "I can hardly believe what I'm hearing. You are going to settle down. Man, I *must* have affected you. So, you gonna marry her in Italy? Will the Army let you do that?"

"Naw, I'll wait till this is all over. Besides, I got some real deals cookin' between me, supply, and the locals, if you know what I mean," he winked.

"Don't get yourself in trouble. That black market crap isn't worth it."

"It's only black if someone is gettin' hurt, Pete. War is hell. And who said anything about the black market? I got honor now," Joey smiled. "Well, gotta go. You comin?"

"Naw, I forgot. I'm pulling guard duty tonight."

"Awe, come on, Peter. You're my lucky man. Make Miller do it."

"No, you go. And don't do anything I wouldn't do," Peter grinned.

"Hey. It's a new Joey Cipriano. I'm so clean I'll probably start being *lucky* without you tagging along," he laughed. "Don't keep the lights on." Joey headed out of the dugout with his GI issue mussett bag.

"What's that for? You aren't planning an overnighter are you?"

Joey rubbed his fingers together and smiled. "I got a few axles to grease. See ya later."

Peter felt uneasy, unsure if he should have let Joey go so easily. If he got caught without a pass, Joey could probably grease the palms of a few MP's and be okay. But something else bothered him.

Artillery sounded in the distance. The Sixth Armored Infantry was taking some real punishment up on the front lines. In a strange way, he wished he were up there. He wanted to get this thing over with and go home to Anna. Sitting around getting shelled wasn't his idea of winning a war.

It had been more than six months since Uncle Billie passed away. He couldn't imagine him dead. This damnable war had taken everyone he loved away from him. At least he had Joey. His friendship had become the closest thing to having a brother he had ever known.

Maybe that was why he felt so uneasy. He wanted to look out for the guy, and he didn't want to lose him. It wasn't about this "luck" thing Joey bantered around all the time. It was something else. A feeling men don't share easily with each other, except in desperate moments.

They were an odd pair. Only the military and the war would have gotten him to hang around a rough and sometimes crude man like Joey certainly could be. Growing up under the influence of Uncle Billie on a small island, he hadn't had much city influences, the kind Joey seemed to revel in. The two were like night and day in personality, but brothers they were. He could count on Joey with his life. They'd both proved that to each other.

"Miller," he called out.

"Yeah, Sarge?" answered his radioman.

"I need a favor from you."

"Yeah?"

"I've got to go into Naples. I'm on guard tonight. You take it for me, and I'll make sure you can count on me for an extra good word with the lieutenant when, you know, you need something."

"Yeah, sure. Okay. I'm doing it for you, not that idiot Joey." Miller knew the score. O'Banyon was watching out for the Italian knothead. "What about Dopey here?" he grinned, pointing to the new crew member with the ears.

"Teach him to run radio, and if the lieutenant asks where Joey and I have gone, just tell him we went for some supplies down in Nettuno. He probably won't question that."

"Gotcha," replied the affable Miller.

"I've got to round up a jeep. Should be back by 1700 hours."

"Roger that, Sarge."

"You're a good man, Miller."

Peter found a Jeep at company mess and traded some of his cigarette rations with the supply sergeant for the six hours he figured he would need it. Cigarettes were like money. Times like this, the cigarettes he didn't smoke anyway came in handy.

It was midday, and the clouds had lifted. The roads where wet, but he figured that with some luck he could catch Joey. He knew Joey would be lumbering down the highway, probably mixing in with some convoy of trucks that streamed supplies up from Naples harbor before returning empty. Naples was a more secure off-loading center for the navy than Anzio beachhead, which allowed the big German guns to reach well out to sea.

He was somewhat concerned about being strafed during an air attack, but he had this gut feeling about catching up with Joey. Uncle Billie had taught him well about instincts, and he had only failed when he didn't follow them. More than once during battle, his instincts saved his tank from disaster.

On such a day as this, the drive along the coast was a mixture of spectacular fraught with misfortune: the kids begging for food, the weary-eyed refugees trying to sort through their bombed-out homes, the awe-inspiring sight of armies and men moving back and forth in coordinated battle plans, now moving into position to attack the ancient city of Rome. It all seemed like a monumental, tragic Greek drama unfolding before him, except he was on stage, too.

Peter was surprised at the relative calm. There was no artillery shelling from the hills above this coastal plain, and no German strafing attacks, although he had seen some enemy planes in the distance headed south. *Probably headed for the Monte Cassino front,* he thought.

He reached the outskirts of Naples without having found Joey's bulging supply truck anywhere in the stream of vehicles he had passed on the highway.

Off to his east, in the hills above the harbor, he thought he saw gun flashes. The Germans used a train track and a flat-bed railroad car to move their big 240-millimeter guns in and out of the mountain tunnels. "Anzio Annie" was what it had become known to those on the receiving end in the beach head to the north. So far, the Air Corps attempts to take these big guns out and Army Ranger raids had all proven fruitless.

When timed between air strikes and bad weather, the huge German artillery shells had hit the big LST's in the harbor, wreaked havoc on convoys, and killed soldiers and civilians alike in indiscriminate barrages on Napoli streets and docks. Peter knew better than to sit still. The gun flashes from the hills had a sound to them now.

He gunned the jeep in a desperate bid to find Joey and get to some underground shelter. One shell screamed over the highway and hit harmlessly in the bay. Ships were coming in. The shells were being fired to correct for effect. Another one screamed over, corrected left one hundred yards, and splashed the hull of a landing craft with sprays of water and shrapnel.

Peter pulled widely in and out of screaming civilians, scurrying for safety amid the rubble-strewn streets. A blast hit the docks just two hundred yards from where he was temporarily stuck in traffic. Soldiers in the convoys were piling out of their trucks and heading for cover.

Another hit, then another, each shell burst occurring closer to the streets that Peter crazily navigated looking for his comrade. Billowing puffs of black smoke issued from some of the vehicles ahead as explosions now rained around him.

Desperate, he zigzagged in and around the debris, anxious to make it to the two hit trucks, just in case.

One was totally lost, engulfed in flames. The other one was hit, but not lost. There was a chance the driver could be alive.

"Joey! Joey . . . No!" he screamed as he skidded to a stop beside the first of the burning trucks. The soldier inside was frantically trying to unjamb the door as the heat from the flames lapped at him. Peter could see that a shell burst had peppered the truck with its hot metallic shards.

But the deadly shelling had stopped as quickly as it had begun. Peter ran to the door, kicked at it, then pulled it as the man inside screamed for help.

The fire wasn't consuming yet, and as he worked to open the door, civilians poured out from everywhere. They came from the buildings and rubble nearest the docks, scampered to the back of the truck, and started to unload its contents, looting it while the driver inside slumped against the door, yelling for someone to rescue him.

Peter screamed and yelled at some of the men to help him, but they avoided the situation as they greedily threw the trucks contents to each other. Peter ran to the jeep to get a crowbar, anything to help him pry open the door.

His anger kindled hotter than the flames issuing from the truck. He grabbed the Thompson submachine gun on the front seat instead of the crowbar and fired a burst over the heads of the scavenging Italians, sending them scurrying from the back of the truck, then he grabbed a tire wretch on the back seat. Another GI came by and began to help.

The soldier inside turned his eyes, wide in an expression of horror, to see his tank crewmember pulling on the hot door handle and yelling for more help.

He put his hands up to the window in a gesture both of surrender and thanks as he slumped against the doorframe.

"Hey, he ain't gonna make it! This thing could blow! Get the hell out of here!" the soldier helping Peter screamed.

As if in slow motion, Peter saw himself screaming and pulling at another truck door many years before. The faces, fresh in his memory, haunted him now . . . his mother, father, and baby sister.

Peter shrugged the soldier off and yelled, "Oh, Lord, my God!" and the door opened as swiftly as the desperate prayer had tumbled from his lips. Joey crumpled onto him, clothes scorched.

He picked the big Italian up in his arms and ran to the cover of the nearby rubble as shells from the German 88's opened up again.

"Hey, what you doin' here?" Joey grimaced, trying for a smile as Peter cradled his head in his lap.

"I've got to look out for you. We're a team," Peter answered, tears falling unashamedly from his eyes.

"You get this stuff in the truck to this address for me?" Joey fumbled as he tried to reach into his battle-fatigue pockets for the slip of paper. "It's for the kids, for the kids . . . food, clothes, blankets," he struggled.

Joey's hands, arms, and legs were seriously burned. "Hey, you don't worry. I'm here. Lucky Peter O'Banyon, right?"

"I don't feel so good. Like Clamser, huh," Joey smiled and began to shake uncontrollably.

"No. Clamser was in bad shape," Peter tried, smiling back.

"My chest hurts," Joey observed as he gritted his teeth.

Peter frantically ripped open his friend's shirt to find blood oozing from a sharp shrapnel wound in his left side. "I gotta get you to an aid station," Peter huffed as he stood with the Italian in his arms.

Joey shivered, gurgled a throaty plea, then relaxed and looked up into Peter's eyes and smiled. "You lucky . . . Pete. I love . . . love Pete."

Sergeant O'Banyon sat there and cradled the man in his arms, rocking him back and forth. The Italian from Jersey City looked at Peter with a wide-eyed sense of amazement at what was happening to him and then relaxed—his eyes rolling back, his mouth open.

"I'm sorry, Joey. I tried to save you. Dammit, Joey, don't do this! Come on, Joey! Joey, I need you! Come on, Joey!"

The shelling stopped again. A medic ran to the soldiers huddled together in the debris and looked for signs of life. He shook his head and then went on to a wounded civilian nearby.

"I swear to God, I'll make them pay for this, Joey," Peter raged without shame as he held the limp head of his companion to his chest. "I swear I'll even this score! I swear! Come on, Joey. I'll take you back."

He picked the tank driver up and loaded him into the jeep for the ride home.

36

SERGEANT O'BANYON got back to Anzio on schedule at 1700 hours.

"Where's Joey?" Miller asked innocently. "What's up with your hands, Sarge?"

Peter offered him an unemotional glance. "Joey's in the morgue." He looked at his bandaged hands, forgetting the burns that he received pulling Joey from the fire. "It's nothing," he answered, holding them up to inspect.

"What? In the morgue, as in . . . dead?" Miller stumbled back, not comprehending.

"Yeah," Peter grumbled, not wanting to lose composure now.

"How?"

"Kraut 88. Direct hit on the truck. Naples. We got orders yet?"

"Yeah," Miller offered shakily. "The lieutenant said we're moving out tonight. Going up to where the sixth has punched a hole in the line. Some village near here. About ten miles northeast, I think."

"You drive. Tell 'Dopey' he's radioman. I load and fire the 75's," Sergeant O'Banyon announced coldly.

"I've only driven twice before," Miller said.

"You'd better learn in a hurry. Just remember what we did at El Guettar in Tunisia. Remember how Joey handled it. We are going to knock out some more of those lousy Panzer SOB's tomorrow, just like we did at El Guettar . . . for Joey," he added.

Miller had never seen a look of complete callousness in the placid sergeant before. "I'm sorry about Joey, Sarge."

"Yeah."

The early morning hours found the tank platoon lined up in an olive grove with the town of Campoleone in the distance. The platoon of twelve Sherman medium tanks was flanked by 105 howitzers. O'Banyon's tank sat in dead center.

"Commence firing," came the order. The entire hillside rocked with shells raining down on the German defenders as the Sixth Infantry moved forward.

"Sarge . . . Lieutenant Kirby on the line," the new radioman said, passing the radio handset up to Sergeant O'Banyon in the turret.

"Sergeant O'Banyon, this is Kirby. I'm sorry we lost Joey. I know its hard being short-handed with just the three of you. If you would like to be relieved, stay back in reserve, I'll understand."

"No, sir, I want this."

"Okay then. You are going to be the point. You will draw fire along with the tanks on your immediate right and left flanks. As you do, our entire right flank will pivot around to the east of town. You maintain a direct course for the highway leading into the village center, understood?"

"Roger. Understood."

"Once we draw enemy fire on you, we will zero in with our spotters and eliminate them, flank the Krauts on the right and while they're busy reinforcing that flank we'll charge in with Dobson and his squad from the north and west and close the door on the highway out of town. Looks like they've got some Tigers we'll be mixing it up with."

"Roger."

"Once this initial barrage ends, you have your orders. I know you are doing double duty as a loader . . . Well, Sergeant O'Banyon, good luck. See you in the village square when this is over."

"Yes, sir. Good luck to you too, sir. Let's kill some Germans and get this over with."

The tank's gears put the armored attackers in motion. The clanking of treads, as they chewed up the soggy earth, and the roar of gasoline-powered engines added to the sounds of hostility the Americans were pouring on the German defenders of Campoleone. Shelling from the division artillery battalion continued unabated, flying over the advancing infantry and tanks and pounding the enemy positions both inside the buildings and surrounding bunkers with devastating effect.

Peter glared through his field binoculars, yelling instructions to the men below him. His hands were greased with petroleum jelly and were hard to move. He wore gloves that would further aggravate the first-degree burns he had suffered the day before in Naples. Loading 75 millimeter shells would make him almost useless by the end of the day.

But he was a man with a mission. He felt nothing but revenge, anger, and hatred for the enemy now. Port Hope Island was a dream that he didn't have time for. This was real, and he wanted the payback for losing Joey.

The enemy started to respond with their own fire now as Panzer tanks moved into position on the ridge line ahead of them. Usually that would give the enemy the advantage, but today the First Armored had air power on their side.

P-38 Mustangs roared over the battle field for the first time in weeks. The cloud cover had hampered their usefulness until today. They strafed the enemy tanks to wake them up and then took pass after pass on the German infantry positions.

The German artillery had located the advancing Americans and, right on cue, had Peter's tank and the two flanking tanks in their gunsights. Three hundred yards, two hundred yards, and now the tanks moved into zigzag maneuvers to avoid becoming bracketed. The Sixteenth Artillery batteries had the enemy locked in, and an artillery duel soon raged, giving Peter's lead tank time to move under the enemy guns in a headlong dash toward the village outskirts.

Murphy's tank on his right was knocked out of action. One, two, three of the men bailed out and headed for cover. An explosion sent the tank cartwheeling over an embankment. That left his and Gunderson's on his left.

On they rolled with infantrymen all around them fighting one-on-one battles; every man, no matter how many other men he was surrounded by, was suddenly alone against the bullets filling the air, the explosions, the cordite drifting across the battlefield.

Peter felt as if he were alone in war. He was the one doing the killing; his men were there just to help him. His tank opened up upon an enemy machine-gun nest five-hundred meters away, in a farmhouse, knocking it out.

They rolled forward through the thundering noise of battle toward their objective. Gunderson's tank on the left exploded, the turret blown off. One of the men jumped out only to be cut down by enemy fire. Sergeant O'Banyon couldn't stop to help the man; he had the objective in sight.

Firing, loading, firing, loading again, he chose to be more than a mere moving target. He yelled at the driver, Miller, to keep going, left, right, forward. Firing as they went, he chose to become a deadly moving menace.

"Scratch one Tiger," he shouted as the enemy tank before him went up in flames.

In front of the infantry now, he received his orders to pull back while the right flank swung into position.

He remembered something Patton had said in North Africa. "Attack, attack, attack. If you are attacking them, they can't attack you. This outfit has retreated for the last time." Sergeant O'Banyon wasn't disobeying the order to pull back, he just couldn't understand it.

The battlefield smoke and low cloud cover moving in from the coast hampered close air support now as well as the artillery spotters. Peter found himself racing toward Campoleone alone. Coming to the realization of the danger he was putting his men under, he pulled his tank into a ravine and contacted the lieutenant.

"Lieutenant Kirby's been wounded," came the voice back through the radio handset.

"What's our situation?"

"Unclear at the moment," came the reply.

Peter contemplated upon his predicament. Probably five-hundred meters ahead of anyone else, including infantry, he'd have to wait for nightfall to pull back safely and hope he wasn't detected in the sandy ravine. *What do I do?* He silently asked himself.

"The unexpected," came the answer, as if whispered to him.

What? He thought. *What was that?* His hearing was suffering from the constant din of firing and explosions.

"Miller, you say something?"

"No, Sarge. But I'd like to," he answered.

"What's that?"

"Let's get the hell out of here," Miller answered.

Peter opened the turret hatch, climbed out of the tank, and walked up to the grassy slope to peer out over the ravine with his binoculars.

The entire battle field had calmed down. He could hear German voices nearby and could see men in front of him running from position to position to set up new defensive perimeters. Approximately three-hundred meters ahead was the edge of town. Behind him he heard the clatter of men and weapons tumbling into the ravine.

"Man, are we glad to see you," one of the soldiers stammered.

"What happened?" Peter asked. "Where's the rest of the Sixth?"

"We got all scattered ta hell and gone. I don't know. There's six of us here. I lost my radioman. You got a radio I can use?"

Peter pointed to the hatch, and the man climbed down in. Coming back minutes later, he broke the news.

"It don't look so good. Most of the tanks and half the trucks got caught in all the mud and mire. How the hell you made it out here is beyond me. But we got one mess on our hands. Seems we're a half a mile ahead of the rest of the force. We either make a stand here or run for it."

"We don't make any stand, and we don't run for it," Peter answered.

"What? You crazy?"

"We do the unexpected. We attack. See that farmhouse over there? Just beyond it is the edge of town. We're taking on that farmhouse. We still got artillery support, don't we?"

"Yeah . . . but . . ."

"Good. We'll direct fire onto that house, take it, then hold until everybody else catches up. The enemy will think we are the main thrust and . . ."

"Kiss us with his 88's. You are crazy," the infantryman replied.

"Look. We're sitting ducks here. I'm not dying out here, okay? I'm going in by myself if I have to. You can crawl back to our lines if you want, but I'm in a war. I got one chance, and that's take them out before they take us out."

The infantryman was a corporal and looked at his squad. They all shrugged their shoulders. "We're probably all dead already. What's the difference?" one of the infantrymen spat back, leaning on his M1 rifle.

"You'd better know what you're doing," said the squad leader and jabbed his finger into Peter's chest.

The tank commander stared at him with eyes of cold steel. "We're going to kill Germans," he declared as he climbed back into the tank.

37

THE DAY wore on into evening. There was no sign of relief nor of counterattack from the enemy. Peter laid a map out with the infantry squad looking on.

"We got one hour to get this right. I've called HQ and given them our position and worked out a plan of escape."

"Escape . . . attack . . . Which is it?" the squad leader barked.

"Both. Look. Things have changed a bit. This damn rain has made the field too muddy for the tracks on this tank. If we take the house, it's got to be a quick surprise. How we got this far in this muck only God knows. We aren't going to be able to move up or back in this stuff. The roads are probably mined, here, here, and here.

"We could make a run with the tank out of the ravine because it's sand, but we have no idea what kind of ambush we'd run into. The patrol you fellas made shows we can drive out the north end of this gully here and swing our gun around and plaster that farmhouse from a direction totally unexpected by the enemy. So far, they don't even know we're out here."

The infantryman shrugged his shoulders. "So what are you suggesting?"

"We got the farmhouse at this location, and this tank is the only 75-milimeter gun this close to it. We have an artillery salvo being directed at the farmhouse at 2100 hours with 105 howitzers, approximately thirty minutes from now. During that barrage, we crank up the engine. The noise from the artillery barrage will cover our tracks. You guys hightail it for the rear while me and my crew add confusion with our 75 rounds and .30-caliber guns. The enemy will be sure to think we're mounting some sort of flank assault. You will have a good chance of making it back to our lines."

"So you never really meant to attack that enemy farmhouse at all?"

"What do you call opening up on it like I just said? Spitin' in the wind? Yeah, we're attacking, doing the unexpected, drawing a diversion. Once they get the drift of what's happening, we bail out and follow you guys. I'm trying to save my crew, and this is the best way I can figure out. Company HQ agrees."

The infantryman smiled. "Man, you're okay. When I saw this tank out here, I thought it was our lucky break. Then I thought you was nuts. With a little luck, this could work," he grinned.

"Luck goes in cycles. Just run like hell when we open up."

38

"WHAT'S GOING on?" Peter groggily asked Private Miller who stood over him.

"You don't remember?"

"Where are we? We made it out of there?"

"Yeah, you sorry lookin' lucky sucker. I thought you was dead," Miller responded.

Peter tried raising his head and looking around the hospital ward. "Seems like we've been here before," he said, trying to crack a smile.

"Yeah," the private offered. "Well, this is it, Sarge. I'm being shipped back to some behind-the-lines job at Division until we get replacements to make up a new tank crew."

"What? What happened after we opened up? That squad get out of there? What happened to the new guy—Dopey, the radioman?"

"The squad made it back okay. You don't remember nothin' about the single First Armored Division tank battle against half of the Hermann Goering Panzer Division?"

"I remember the artillery letting loose, then we opened up, and I remember yelling at you, but that's pretty much it. How about Dopey? What was his name, anyway?"

"Private First Class James Mulligan. He got it."

"An Irishman. Should have paid more attention. It's hard to want to get close to new guys, know what I mean?"

"Yeah, Sarge. I know what you mean."

"So it's just you and me?"

"All that's left, Sarge. You saved my can. I came to thank you."

"Think nothing of it. I'm sure you would've done the same."

"No, Sarge. You pushed me out of the hatch the same way you did back in Tunisia. That's twice. I owe you."

"What happened next?"

"We were running like hell. German machine-gun nest, M40's I think, opened up on us from a clump of bushes somewhere. You threw me into a ditch and took the rounds. You were out cold, blood coming out of your legs, one stomach wound. It didn't look too good. I went for help, and we got you out of there that night. That was a week ago."

"Oh." He lay back staring at the white-washed ceiling. "So what's this place?"

"Some sort of underground hospital in Naples. You're being shipped out with the rest of these guys today. The war's over for you, Sarge."

"Did we ever take Campoleone?"

"No, but we got two enemy Mark VI's confirmed by Division. That farmhouse, too. With all the firing going on, you probably don't remember. But we did. I hear the Division has almost broke the Kraut's line at Cisterna, and they think they'll have the town soon. Man, will I be glad to break out of that godforsaken Anzio. They've been shelling us from those hills pretty bad, and the rain just doesn't stop. Our dugout . . . well, it ain't a pretty sight."

"Never was. Well, Miller, keep your head down. You did a fine job driving the tank."

"Learned from the best."

"Yeah." Peter extended his bandaged hands. "Oh," he said as he held them both up for inspection. "Joey."

"Yeah, Joey." Miller smiled. "Good luck, Sarge. You ever get to Lawrence, Kansas, look me up."

"I'll do that. You ever get to Massachusetts, take a ferry out to Nantucket. From there take a little trawler owned by this guy named Hal. I'll be at a lighthouse on a little island called . . ."

"Yeah . . . Port Hope," he interrupted. "Heard that name somewhere before," he grinned.

Miller waved from the door as he stood there looking a little lost. He was a just a kid.

Peter may as well have been God himself to the nineteen-year-old, the way he counted on him. He had been a kid when this all started almost two years earlier.

"Nurse?"

"Yes, soldier?" the nearby army nurse answered, sticking a thermometer in his mouth.

"How long before we get to the States, the hospital ship, I mean?" he muttered, biting the thermometer between his lips.

"You're not going directly home, Sergeant. First stop is England. There, you'll be in rehabilitation where they'll fix these," she threw back the sheets for him to see his mangled legs. "You're lucky to still have a right foot the way those German bullets ripped into it," she stated matter-of-factly. "The doctor took a lot of muscle tissue from your calf. You're lucky. He was getting ready to amputate when he changed his mind. He said he got a sudden idea and, well, it seems to have worked. You'll need some long rest and then plenty of good exercise before you'll be sent home."

Peter stared at the bloody, oozing sight. "My stomach?"

"They got the bullet. Lodged near the spine. It took a piece of intestine, but you're doing real good. I've seen a lot worse," she smiled, shaking the thermometer. "Welcome back to the world, Sergeant," she remarked clinically and walked away.

Peter closed his eyes. He hated the killing and the loss of Joey and his other Army pals. But he hated another kind of death even more. It was a deep sense of connection, hard to put a finger on. He couldn't figure out what it was. He just knew he wasn't the same. He'd lost his innocence and was cold inside. He hoped Anna would understand.

39

PETER LOOKED out from the top railing of the ocean liner converted to troop transport, the Queen Mary, and could make out the New York skyline. It was almost two years to the day since he married his sweetheart. He tried to comprehend all that had happened in so short a time and what the changes meant.

He marries.

Gets drafted.

Says goodbye to Uncle Billie.

Uncle Billie dies.

He meets Joey and other soldiers.

Fights Germans and Italians in North Africa and Italy.

Gets medals for just doing what he should do.

Friends get killed. Joey dies.

He is a father of a one-year-old child he hasn't met.

He kills people. He saves people.

He is two years older.

How could so much stuff happen in just two years? He wondered. He was different inside and out. The easygoing, happy-go-lucky kid was dead. A more stiff, confident, and fearful man had been born.

But he was glad to be back. He handled the black and white photo of Anna and his baby girl, Kathleen, as he leaned up against the rail. They didn't know he would be coming home this week. He wanted it that way.

An anniversary surprise, he hoped he could get his discharge papers processed in New York and take his thirty-day leave until the discharge orders came through, unmolested by anything and everything. He just wanted peace and to hear the sounds of nothing but the waves breaking on the beach, the gulls screaming in the air, and feel the sun beating on his face while he held his beloved Anna and baby girl in his arms.

The Statue of Liberty was finally in full view. He swore to kiss the ground when he got into the harbor. *Uncle Billie had worked this harbor,* he thought.

"Something in this statue that gets a guy choked up every time I see it," he overhead a sailor say.

Peter looked around at the young and happy faces. Soldiers two and three deep packed and lined the rail. At the sight of the statue a general cheer went up that rocked the boat. The man next to him, in a wheelchair, was crying.

"I'll never leave the United States again as long as I live," he overheard one soldier tell another.

"I'm going to kiss the ground then the first dame I meet," another offered.

"That'll just make her melt into your arms," ribbed an Army buddy.

"Aw, shut up. What she doesn't know won't hurt her."

"Man, I can smell my mama's beef roast now," drawled a Texan.

"You oughta taste this chicken pot pie my mama cooks. Ooh, it's enough ta make a grown man cry," added a Virginian.

"When I get home to Omaha, I'm taking the longest shower in recorded history. Then I'm eating a steak. Then I'm going down to Max's Corner Drug Store for a strawberry malt, then a vanilla, then a chocolate. That's all I been thinking about for weeks," sighed another soldier.

Peter gazed around. Home was within reach. Until now, the belief that home was really theirs, something real, was a reservation they all had kept silent. It was still wartime, and there were submarines in the Atlantic. Like the rest, he had to see to believe.

Believing felt good right now. The loud talking, laughter, hugging, dancing, jocular demonstrations of more than five thousand men aboard ship seemed to propel the troop ship to it's berth.

"Thank you, God. Alive and home. I swear I'll never ask for nothing else as long as I live," Peter whispered under his breath.

40

"PETER, MY God, boy! It's good to have you back!" Hal smiled, proudly patting the young soldier on the back as he helped him with his duffle bag off the trawler and onto the dock.

"It's good to be back, Hal," Peter answered, taking in a deep breath as he did. "I'm home. God in Heaven, thank you," he prayed unashamedly as his eyes took in the sight. "Hal, I'm home!" he grinned broadly as he leaned on his walking cane.

"Anna doesn't know you're coming home today?" Hal asked for the upteenth time, looking for something to say.

"It should be quite a surprise, huh?"

"Let me drive you up there, Peter," he hurried, grabbing the bag.

"Tell ya what, Hal. I need the walk. I need it bad, and I want to savor this, walking this road like I did as a kid. I can't

228

carry this bag that far yet. If you would bring it up for me, oh, say in an hour, that would be swell."

"You got it. And, Peter, your Uncle Billie was mighty proud of you. Mighty proud. He sure is smiling down on you. I know it."

"Uh . . . yeah. Sure. Thanks," Peter choked out a throaty response, caught off guard by the emotions which swept through him suddenly. *Uncle Billie wouldn't be there to greet me.* . . . It was suddenly real now. "See ya in an hour, Hal," he waved and began the two-mile walk up the gentle slope to the lighthouse.

It was June 4, and the wire services in Boston already had the news. The Allies had entered Rome. He would have been there if not for the wound, not that he wasn't glad to be home, but after all the fighting and killing, he deserved to at least see the "Eternal City." Maybe he would take Anna there after the war—a belated honeymoon.

This air is the freshest air on earth, he thought as he deeply drank and filled his lungs with it.

Home. *What will she look like? Will she be angry at me for not telling her how bad my wounds really were? Will my little girl be frightened of me? What should my first words to her be?*

He smiled as his mind filled with the pleasant memories of boyhood that every rock, every flower in the meadow, seemed to bring back. He stopped and looked into the grassy field and saw a small boy there, flying a kite. It could have been him.

"Uncle Billie, look!"

"Aye, that's my boy. Good lad. Now hold her steady and let a wee bit of string out at a time."

Mesmerized by the flood of recollections, he let go a heavy sigh of relief and gratitude. "Thank you, Uncle Billie," he whispered and began his walk again.

The lighthouse was in view now. He picked up his pace to match the brisk beating of his heart. His legs surged with new-found strength as he made his way, faster—now just feet from the door. Should he knock? Should he call out her name?

He peered through the window. No one. He tried the door handle. It opened to the familiar scents of his former life, real life! He closed his eyes and took it in.

"Anna?" he called out meekly. "Anna, darling?"

No answer. But they were home. Food was on the table; some toys were on the floor. He picked one up. A Raggedy Ann doll. He smiled and placed it gently on the sofa.

He left the door open as he turned and walked out across the meadow to the beach stairs that led down to the pier in the cove. His heart filled with anxiety. This is the place he dreamed about a thousand times. What if she wasn't there? What if she was?

"Anna! Anna!" he called, waving the cane over his head. "Its me. I'm home," he cried as he saw his wife holding their daughter on the pier.

She arose startled. Not willing to believe her ears, she stood there frozen, her back to him. "Say something again. Dear God, make me believe it's really him," she whispered softly. Her baby bolted in her arms, turning her head around. She knew.

"Anna . . ." he called, cupping his hands to his mouth. He waved his cane again and then, throwing it to the ground, started down the stairs like a man desperate for a breath of life.

She ran to the stairs with their baby and met him at the base. They stared first—eyes filling with moisture, heads nodding.

"It's me," he said softly, creasing his somber lips with the smile she remembered.

She put her hand to her face, tears streaming profusely off her cheeks.

He wept as he stood frozen, gazing at the two most beautiful women in the world. She came to him, falling into his arms.

"Peter, darling, you're home. . . . Oh, sweetheart, you're home," she cried, overcome with the joy and surprise his sudden appearance caused.

He whispered in her ear. "Happy anniversary, Anna. Thank you for being such a good lighthouse keeper, darling. I knew you could do it. You brought me home, and I'm home for good."

41

I'M SORRY I didn't tell you a lot of things, Uncle Billie," he said softly as he knelt at the grave behind the lighthouse. "I want to say them now. I understand what you tried to tell me about being not just a lighthouse keeper, but a lightkeeper. It got me through this. And I love you. Thank you, Uncle Billie. Amen." He wiped at his face and got up to hear his baby, Kathleen, say, "Daddy!" as she ran to him for the first time on her own initiative.

Anna took in the joyful scene as she realized Kathleen had connected the photos of "Daddy in the Army" she had showed her nightly before prayer time.

They walked into the quiet cottage, arm and arm. Kathleen, tired now, nuzzled up to her daddy and fell asleep on his shoulder.

"What do I do?" He laughed, not ever having handled a child before.

"Here," Anna smiled as she gently lifted their baby daughter from him and tenderly placed her in the crib by the large bay window.

They sat, looking into each other's eyes and holding hands; he rubbing hers, she responding to the gentleness of his rough hands.

She grabbed at each one of his hands with each of hers, turned them palm up and gasped at the pinkish color, the scars.

"I tried to save Joey," he simply explained to the questioning look in her eyes.

A flood of unexpected emotions gripped him. His lips quivered as he attempted to speak. "The street, Naples. We were being hit bad, real bad. Joey's truck got hit and, well. . . ." He couldn't say anything more. Head bowed, he fought the water dripping from his eyes onto his uniform. "I tried to save him. That's all." There was quiet as she held his hands, watching him struggle to mentally come home to her.

"Look," he brightened. "They move pretty good now," he smiled, half-heartedly holding his fingers up to move them for her.

She embraced him, putting her tender skin against his so he could feel her warmth. "I'm here, and you'll never leave me again."

"I swear, Anna, I will never leave you again. I swear I'll stay right here, and we'll raise our kids until we are so old and so gray we can't recall who we are," he offered, finally clearing his throat.

"Me, too," she said, brushing her hands across his stubbled cheeks.

"You'd look handsome with a beard, a short and trim one, of course."

"Maybe I should grow one, now that I'm the official light-house keeper."

"Are you hungry?"

"For more than food," he breathed, bringing her lips up to meet his.

"Then let's eat," she softly said, guiding his hands.

Hal smiled. He should have known better than to knock. He left the duffle bag at the door and walked around to the back meadow to visit Billie O'Banyon.

"Well, Billie. Your boy is home. A fine man he is. A hero, too. I'm just about done with my work for today and thought I'd say hello. Don't come up here as regular as I should. Just thought you should know there's a lighthouse keeper back to work."

The island's jack-of-all-trades, tipped his hat and walked back happily to his motorbike with sidecar, leaving the hill and the lovers to their reunion.

42

BOSTON COLLEGE COMMENCEMENT
MAY 1949

ANNA REACHED up to her husband and kissed him as
caps flew in the air. "Congratulations, honey," she smiled,
offering a long and lingering kiss.

Kathleen tugged at his pant leg while her parents embraced.
"Daddy," she tugged. "Daddy!" she yelled above the raucous-
ness of the celebrating throng of graduating class members and
their families. "Congratulations," she smiled, proud of her ac-
complishment in spiting the big word out.

"Thank you, sweetheart," he returned as he picked his four-
year-old up and held her tightly. "Well, it's time. A three
month Port Hope Island vacation. No school for three
months," he smiled.

"I'm so proud of you, sweetheart," Anna said holding his
hand as they walked toward their new 1948 Dodge converti-

ble. "Life is so good," she breathed deeply. "Harvard Law School. I can hardly believe it," she added.

"Me, too," he said as they walked hand in hand. "You don't think three more years is a bit much?" he asked hopefully.

She knew what it meant to him. After the war, all he talked about was contributing in some way, making the world better, doing something to help people. He thought law, maybe even politics, might be a way to contribute to peace and the betterment of the world.

"Uncle Billie would be proud. That money he set aside for us and for the kids' education is being used the right way. I want this for all of us," she encouraged in reply.

"Kids," Peter sighed. "Well, I guess we can spend the summer trying a bit harder. Not much to do out there on the island," he grinned.

She offered a willing pat to the seat of his graduation gown. "Maybe this time," she smiled back to him.

"What did the doctor say?" he asked seriously.

"He said he sees no reason why I can't conceive and that maybe you should be checked out, though. He says he's seen more than one veteran come home, and the wife doesn't conceive, but they don't have any evidence of anything wrong . . . nothing scientific."

He nodded as they reached the car door. "I wasn't wounded below the beltline, except below the knees," he reassured her.

"I know. Come on, let's go home and see what we can do about it."

They arrived late to the island home, and Peter lit the powerful parabolic lamp, the last of its kind on the coast.

"It's a beautiful night. The moon is out. Want to take a moonlight dip?"

"Maybe," she flirted, dropping the strap off one of her shoulders.

"Will she be okay sleeping?" Peter whispered.

"She'll be fine for half an hour. Look at her. She's all worn out. Let me grab my bathing suit," she answered.

"Why?" he teased, bringing her up to him so he could nuzzle her tender neck.

"Because. That's why. Now, go get yours," she slapped at him in mock struggle.

"I'll race you," he laughed, looking down at his battle-scarred legs.

"No, we'll take this nice and slow. Isn't it gorgeous?" she asked, pointing to the full moon aided by a thousand stars lighting the calm waters of the bay. They walked hand in hand down to the beach and fell into the soft white sand, kissing as they did.

"I love you," he whispered, tickling her ear with his gentle words.

"I want to hear that the rest of my life. The last words I want to hear from those lips," she smiled, "today, tomorrow, always."

"I love you, I love you, I love you," he added between each kiss as he moved down from her lips to her neck.

She got up suddenly and ran to the pier, teasing him. "Come on. You chicken?"

"Me? Chicken? Tank Commander Peter O'Banyon afraid of a little cold water?" he scoffed. "But I was just getting warmed up," he added, encouraging her to come back to the towel spread out on the beach.

Anna ran down to the end of the pier and dove in. "Come on, darling. I have a surprise," she laughed.

"That's encouragement enough," he yelled back.

They swam and played and felt the love they had for each other, joyfully, playfully, for longer than they had intended to stay out. A higher tide was coming when they heard a child's voice.

"Mommy? Daddy? Where are you?" their child's voice cried with an accompanying splash near the fishing pier and boat-dock.

"Oh God, No! Peter," Anna cried as the tide began to surge in unexpected waves against the pilings of the long boatdock.

They both swam furiously toward the end of the pier, filled with adrenalin, diving under the water near the end.

"I can't find her!" he yelled, coughing out water and taking another deep breath to go under the water again.

"Me neither. Oh, Peter!" Anna cried as she treaded water and swam toward him. "I'll take this side," she called out in a terrified voice above the noise of the increasing lapping of waves against the barnacled pilings which supported the tiny boatdock.

"Kathleen! Baby, where are you?"

"Here, Daddy," she called back, crying. "I falled in. I want mommy," she cried, standing near the front of the pier in knee-deep water.

"Here we go, sweetheart," Peter said, grabbing her and putting her safely onto the shore. Sit right here. I'll go get mommy." He ran back out, calling for Anna.

"Anna, honey, she's safe. I found her. It's okay. Come on in, Anna," he cupped his hands calling her against the sounds of the waves beating harder against the pilings.

"Anna, answer me!" he yelled louder this time. Panic swept through him as he searched the pier on the side Anna had taken to look for their daughter. He ran to the end of the pier and screamed, "Anna!" No answer.

He dove in and swam frantically around and under the pier looking for her. "My God! Don't do this!" he spit out as he took in another deep breath. "Don't let this happen!" he said and dove under the water again.

The moonlight illuminated the crystal waters of the cove as he swam in and out of the pilings. He searched each one, desperately holding on to his breath for as long as he could with each dive.

Kathleen was crying. "Stay there, baby," he cried, shaken by the awfulness of what was happening to them. "I got to find mommy," he called out with a broken voice, only making Kathleen more hysterical. "Stay. Don't move," he commanded his daughter firmly as he pulled himself up to the pier. He ran up and down calling for Anna then dove back in the water, crying out for her.

"Anna! Dear God . . . Anna, answer me!" The tide was coming in, pushing the bottom of the sandbar beyond the reach of his toes. He was treading water, knowing that if she were unconscious she could be pulled out to sea. Kathleen's cry, "Daddy, Mommy, where are you?" filled him with desperation.

"Anna, don't do this!" He struggled against exhaustion. He felt his arm and leg muscles tighten as he gasped for air, lungs burning for more oxygen. *One more dive*, he thought as he ducked under the pier and a wave crashing against the pilings.

The wave knocked him violently into the barnacled supports of the boatdock, causing a gash to his head and stunning him dizzily. He knew he had to live for Kathleen. His last desperate move needed to be for his crying baby.

He pulled himself onto the pier thoroughly exhausted and spent, gasping for air and praying at the same time.

"Don't take her from me! Dear Jesus, don't let this happen! I need her! Please," he begged as he lay flat on the boardwalk, spiting sea water from his mouth, having done all his energy would allow him to do.

Gathering himself to his knees, fully aware that if he found her now, with the time that had elapsed, it was unlikely that she would have survived. He called out for her in desperation. "Anna! . . . Anna, baby . . . answer me! God in heaven, don't do this!" he yelled against the cries of his little girl who ran to him now.

Letting out all the air from his lungs in one final heaving effort, he screamed her name, "Anna!"

43

I T WAS a sick, perverse joke perpetrated on him by a sick, perverse god of Greek proportions. Like Zeus, the whimsical deity of the ancients, someone was pulling his strings so that fate had all say in the drama, and he, Peter, had none. He bitterly watched as the casket was lowered into the ground next to Billie's grave.

I've never really saved anyone, have I? He numbly posed the question to himself.

His parents, Joey, even Clamser, finally died; two other crew members, Myers and what's his name, Dopey, the new guy; Uncle Billie, when he needed him most, Peter was away; now Anna.

Peter O'Banyon had seen enough of death, and he was sure of one thing, nobody the angel of death touched ever came back. He looked at his daughter being held by Anna's tearful mother. Kathleen was too young to understand the impact. She would never know her mother. Not really.

The gathering at the service was beyond feelings of grief.

The sorrow of Anna's family, mixed with that of the islanders, caused the quiet suffering of one, combined with the next, and the next person attending the mournful scene, to create a general moan which rose upwards to condemn God, or at least to plead for understanding.

He didn't pray, and he didn't want to understand. He just wanted Anna back. He didn't leave the island six years earlier to go off and fight a war to come home and lose all that he lived for, all that had helped him survive.

She was too good, too kind, too loving to die. She was what the world needed, and it hurt to see the brown oak box with her limp remains lowered into the cold earth, never to come back.

They had combed the cove the next day, and it was Hal, with his trawler, who found Anna's body floating beyond the breakers, pulled away from the cove by a riptide.

The after-service social began. Now there were the hugs, the tears, the photo-album reviewing, the casseroles provided by the woman's group from the church they attended on Nantucket. He would be glad when it was over.

Should he stay on here at the lighthouse? *What was the purpose in it anyway?* he had wondered as the minister said the dedication prayer at the grave. What would he do without her?

Well-intended things were said to try to lift his spirits. Anna's parents were the final ones to leave, and they offered to take Kathleen for the week while Peter stayed behind to close up the lighthouse.

He kissed his baby girl and promised to see her soon and waved good-bye as Hal took his last load of passengers down the hill in the delivery truck for the ferry ride to Nantucket and beyond.

Peter looked around him. The celebration of Anna's life was over. It had helped some, he guessed, but he loved her as much in her death as he ever had in her life. To him it felt like the war again.

Like the war, separation was a circumstance that had to be dealt with. Now death, a totally permanent circumstance, had taken her from him.

He rummaged through the photos and then lost control, falling to the sofa, clutching at his stomach for an end to the gut-wrenching seizure that was controlling him. He was utterly and completely lost without her.

At length, he sat up, not knowing what to do with himself. He was angry at God. *Shouldn't I be? Or was it God who had let me come home from the war to be with her for a short while? Maybe a merciful God . . .*

If he could just die. . . . Kathleen was young enough to bounce back. He could walk out to sea and just end it.

He left the lighthouse behind as he tearfully wandered, head bent low in sorrow, to the stairway leading to the beach, the pier, and what no one in the world could blame him for, his end.

He stood there watching the sun set off to the west, outlining the faint shoreline of Nantucket. He could be dead in ten, fifteen minutes he guessed, if he just had the courage to do it.

He slowly took each step down the switchback stairs Uncle Billie had constructed two decades earlier. His legs, weighted with the same sorrow of his heart, drew him there, to the pier. They had been so happy just days before, so full of life and hope for the future.

Standing on the end of the pier, he gazed into the murky depths. *Just step off,* an angry inner voice prompted. *Just do it.*

He stared in disbelief that life could come to this, but as he did, his mind went back and reflected all his longings for the wife of his youth in the mirrorlike waters.

Their letter writing, their longing for each one, their promise to share the experiences written in his diary. . . . *For what?*

"It helps me keep a hold ta what I cherish most, laddie," he recalled his Uncle Billie answering when Peter asked why he kept the lighthouse logbook up-to-date.

The log book . . . where is it, anyway? His thoughts shifted with the question. *Anna said she had it stored in a box. I always meant to go through Uncle Billie's stuff but never had the heart,* he mumbled to himself.

He raised his gaze away from the silvery surface of the water to avoid his own reflection. The setting sun changed the water's mood from silvery blue to shimmering aquamarine. The last rays of light gave rise to thoughts of Uncle Billie, smiling, laughing, scolding but always caring for him. He closed his eyes to drink deeply of the memory of the man and . . .

"The logbook!" he whispered under his breath.

"Aye, the logbook," a forceful and familiar voice said to him.

He spun around to see who was there.

Imagination. That was all. But he started walking up the stairs from the beach to the crest of the hill above.

Like a man possessed, he ran to the lighthouse and swung the door open wide. "Where did she store it?"

"Attic above the closet," a voice spoke in his head. He stumbled to the hall closet and grabbed a stool, stepping up and pushing open the attic trapdoor. He peered inside the area, large enough for just a few boxes and other stored items. He moved Kathleen's cradle to one side and grabbed for the box marked "Billie," pulling it down with him to the living room.

Opening its folded corners, there, laying on top of Uncle

Billie's most cherished personal items, was the old, black, leatherbound lighthouse log.

Peter blew the dust off and let the book fall open. Wedged on a page marked "May 13, 1943" he found a sealed onionskin envelope. Never opened, it was addressed to Peter from Uncle Billie, and it had occupied the space in the lighthouse log as if it had waited for this moment.

Peter ripped at it gently, anxious to read words written from the grave. Several pages fell out of the envelope. He picked them up and leaned back into the afghan-covered sofa and read.

He read hungrily, like a man looking for whatever he had lost, hoping to find it. Tears burned his eyes, blurring his vision as he did. The answers to all he had questioned these last days were outlined as if written for this moment.

He read, reread, and read the message again, the last words Uncle Billie had written him, intended for the day he got home from the war but lost in the excitement of his homecoming.

He closed his eyes, trying to believe and comprehend what Uncle Billie was telling him. After some time of ponderous silence, he allowed the pages to become a part of him. As if in soliloquy, he released a heavy sigh that allowed the past to be buried. "I loved her, God. That's why I couldn't let her go. But now I *can* thank you . . . for allowing her to be in my life at all."

He opened his eyes and saw the sun emerge from behind a cloud, and everything around him was suffused with healing light.

44

"DAD, I'M so sorry for all you went through for me," Kathleen offered sadly as he finished his storytelling. "I took mom away from you, didn't I?"

"Oh, no! You were her joy, sweetheart. And mine, too. There must be a good reason for all things," he answered kindly.

"Dad, the sun is setting in about an hour. It's so beautiful, isn't it?" Kathleen offered, paint brush in hand, seated next to him with her easel to one side. "If I could just finish this scene for you . . ."

Peter struggled to look at her painting, the gift she had worked so diligently to produce for his final days. "It is like a living picture of this place. So wonderful . . . You've captured it, sweetheart," he coughed. "I'm getting sleepy," he said matter-of-factly.

246

"Shall we go in, Dad?"

"Will you turn the light on once more and let me see it like I want to remember it?"

"Okay, Dad," she leaned toward him and gently kissed his cheek. He was wrapped in a blanket with the logbook firmly in his grip. "I'll just run on down to the docks to pick up some paints from my friend. She has some colors I think I need for this pier scene. Then I'll be right back and turn on the light and we can watch day turn to night together. Be right back."

"I love you, Kathleen," he called to her with great earnestness and effort.

She froze in her steps, thinking she should stay with him. "I love you, too, Dad. Be right back. Twenty minutes tops," she called. "Looks like a fog is rolling in. I'll hurry."

He waved her on with a shaky hand gesture and looked out to the ocean he had loved so well. It never changed. He was grateful for that.

His eyes grew wide at the light, wider than he thought he could open them. *So soon?* he wondered. *Kathleen could not have fired up the lighthouse so quickly.* It brilliantly lit the pier and cove with a luminescence he never recalled the lighthouse lamp having caused before.

There was someone on the pier waving to him. A young man he once knew. . . . He could swear it. He continued waving to Peter.

He struggled to get out of the wheelchair and wave back. The man was confusing him. "Joey?" he whispered as he struggled to stand.

What is he doing here?

It was no use. The body he was trapped in was too wooden for his weakened arms to raise him to his feet.

Peter looked down at the logbook in his lap. *It is all here, isn't it? My life, the stories? Uncle Billie's?*

He looked up from his lap and back down to the pier as the fog rolled over it, obscuring his vision. He couldn't believe what he was seeing.

Lifelike figures from his memory came out from the fog. He wondered about it with the mind of a child taking his first lessons in addition or subtraction. The images seemed to be moving about upon the fog-shrouded pier. First one, then two, now three. Illusions. They must be simply that. Drifting in and out of the mist.

He sat there mystified at what was happening, feeling very dreary in body from the vigil he had endured these two days, but he felt light of mind, a sleepy lightness.

His eyes seemed to blur in their focus now, and he knew that sleep was soon to come upon him.

But, dear God, not until I see her once more, he thought. If I leave this island without seeing my beloved once more. . . . He had her in life once. *Just one more time, bring her to me,* he begged.

Peter wanted the dream to come true like a child wanting a fantasy, an innocent dream, to become real, to become fully material and touchable. He longed for his release to that dream world now, but only if she would be found there, forever holding him. Then he could go home.

His eyes, heavy and longing for this singular event, lifted from the old logbook to the scene below.

"Clamser?" he trembled as he squinted into the lifting fog. The illusion appearing on the pier was joined by two others. "Miller? Olsen?" They all looked up at him now. They seemed to be enjoying themselves, talking like they did in North Africa and Italy. They seemed so real, waving to him to join them.

His eyes filled with glassy wetness, and he turned, desperately fumbling to the final page of the lighthouse logbook to make sure the letter was there, the final letter from Uncle Billie. *Okay, everything is going to be okay,* he thought.

He lifted his eyes once more and found himself running down the grassy slope, a nineteen-year-old again, the way it had been in 1942. He reached the steps to the pier and stopped, expecting his dream to vanish, causing him to awaken.

"How's my lucky charm?" one of the smiling young soldiers said as he walked toward Peter.

"Joey?" Peter's mouth fell agape as he stepped onto the pier. "Joey? You're . . . you look so alive . . . so good!" Peter laughed with all the energy of his youth. He ran to meet his long ago army brother.

The two tank-crew members embraced. Peter wept. But he was sure he would awake from this dream, as he had so many dreams before. This was just the vivid imaginings of a tired old man who had spent two days relating his life with these men to his daughter. *The drugs . . . it must be the pain killers,* he thought.

He looked up and down, examining himself and his hands. "My hands!" he exclaimed like a little boy discovering something for the first time. They weren't marked by the scars of war anymore, and he moved them as easily as he had in his schoolboy days.

He tilted his head back and let out a loud, hearty, youthful laugh. *This dream feels good,* he thought, smiling at the apparition before him. He reached out to touch its face.

The soldier smiled back at him.

"I know that smile! I know you!" He laughed again in wonder. Then Peter looked deeper into the penetrating blue eyes and read his thoughts. "I tried to save you, Joey. I did try," he muttered quietly as they drew closer to each other. He buried his head in the ample arms of his big Italian brother.

"You did save me," Joey replied, smiling. Like a proud father would to his son, he grasped Peter's shoulders and inspected him. He nodded approvingly and then stepped back for another image to come forward.

"Clamser? I thought you didn't make it," Peter voiced.

The soldier from World War II replied. "I made it long enough to get home and see my wife and kids . . . to tell them the most important three words I could. It meant a lot to them over the years. I've come to thank you." They embraced and he, too, fell back.

"Miller from Kansas? And Olsen from Iowa?"

"We both lived long and happy lives because of you, Sarge. You saved me twice," Miller said.

"I always meant to say thank you for pulling me out of there at Gafsa. I was too angry about my football days being over, about losing my leg, about never running again, to write and tell you," a more awkward and shy Olsen said as he stepped forward.

"Olsen, . . . you . . . you got your leg back?" Peter asked like a child discovering something wonderful for the first time.

"Sure did. Good as new, too, Sarge. See?"

Peter stood there, more sure than ever that this was the sweet dream deserved for enduring so many years alone and wondering, hoping he had made a difference somewhere.

He expected Kathleen to wake him as he stood there smiling at all four men, like it were yesterday at the battles that had made them brothers.

"We've been assigned to escort you home," Joey said, stepping forward. "So, this is the island paradise you bragged about so much," he said, not able to restrain the old Joey inside him.

"I've got to go back to the lighthouse and tell my daughter something. I've got to wake up and . . ." he said pointing up to the beam that now radiated from the lighthouse onto the pier.

"My little girl, she must have turned the light on. She said she would do it one more time for me," Peter remonstrated at Joey's insistence that they leave now. "She does this at sunset so I can think about . . ."

Peter's eyes turned from staring into the brilliant light to where it shone on the pier. The soldiers stood aside. The fog had lifted entirely, and there was no ambiguity in what his eyes beheld . . . and what feeling radiated from inside him.

Anna had her back to him as if she were gazing far out to sea, waiting for something or someone.

He looked back up the hill and there sat, slumped in the chair, a lonely old man full of dreams. He turned quickly back to the pier, and she spun around to face him.

"Anna? . . . Anna!" he screamed as he boyishly ran to her.

"I love you, darling! Oh, I love you!" she wept as he embraced and twirled and held her like a man holding on for dear life.

"Anna, Anna, sweetheart. Anna, darling! I don't want you to leave me. Don't let me wake up, please?" he cried like a little boy in fear as she wiped at his tears.

I'm real. You're real, and they're real, she thought to him joyfully. She pointed beyond the pier, and the lighthouse beam seemed only to grow brighter as it illuminated two people walking toward them.

A happy man, in his early thirties, and a startling lookalike to his own Anna, walked together arm in arm, laughing, smiling, healthy, alive. . . .

"Anna?" Peter's eyes grew wide. "Am I . . . are we . . . ?"

She drew herself up to him, pressed the soft skin of her dimpled cheeks against his face, and whispered as she kissed him, "We are more alive than we have ever been."

The happy couple drew closer. The man stopped, then smiled, and opened his arms, and called to him. He'd heard that voice before, but the last time was June 6, 1942, the day he shipped off to war.

"Do ya know me, laddie?"

"Aye," Peter called back happily, loudly, tears coursing down his face. His lips creased into a wide grin of recognition. The man drew nearer as Peter stepped off the pier with Anna and anxiously ran toward him.

"Peter, lad, I've missed ya. I've come ta take ya home."

Epilogue

KATHLEEN HURRIED up the road from the Port Hope docks. She had only been gone for one-half hour, a little longer than she promised, but she wondered at the light. Surely her father couldn't have made his way up the stairs to turn it on. A strange foreboding, surreal sensation enveloped her as she stopped the car and raced across the meadow to where her father sat.

"Dad," she called, stopping short of his chair. "Dad?" she asked again gently.

Her heart paced to a sprinter's beat as she walked the remaining steps to his side with the heaviness of leaden legs. They feared what they might bring her to.

She squatted down in front of his chair and looked up to his face, head slumped down, chin lying upon his emaciated chest. "Oh, Dad!" she cried, not wanting this moment to be, to come like this. She sobbed, kissing his cheeks and vainly hoping he would, could arouse to life to at least say good-bye.

She wiped at her burning eyes—tears dropping like rain upon the book in his lap. The pages fluttered in a light breeze. She noticed his shaky, cursive hand and his final logbook entry made the day before. She had a part of him now.

She took the time-withered yellow envelope that marked the page and which held inside its folds a faded onionskin letter. The letter, marked clearly by the wear of years and a thousand readings, evidenced by the smudged fingerprints fraying its edges, was written over fifty years before. She had never read it but had promised her father she would some-day . . . upon this occasion.

She sat next to him on the thick carpet of field grass. There was no hurry now, no urgency. Wiping at her eyes with the back of her hand, she wanted just a moment, like this, her final one with the lighthouse keeper.

Unfolding the aged creases, she pulled the letter closer to her moist and stinging eyes and began to read:

May 13, 1943

My dear son Peter,

For you are a son to me, and I love ya like your Da always did. I bequeath all I have to you. You will find my estate is in order, and you and your beloved shall never want for anything.

But what I have to say to you is far more important and fills my old mind with urgency as I ponder on it. Maybe I shall be alive after this war, when you return, and maybe I shall not. So I write it all here for ya to ponder on.

This life is a shadowy thing, lad. We live in a crowded

space of lights and shadows, and when left to ourselves, we all too often fail to see the brightest light of all.

I learned from a woman I loved, long ago, how to get the most from life—from love. She it was who taught me the symbolism in lightkeepin',' though she never set foot on this tiny speck of sand in the great Atlantic coasts. She came to me in a dream not a fortnight ago. She stood before me as fair as the day I first met her, and I was so proud for havin' waited for her to come to me.

She held out her hand and touched mine, and I knelt at her blessed feet and wept like a little child. I heard her speak to me, and these were the words she spake:

"William, we have a light upon our house, and it gives hope to all who sail upon the stormy seas. Do ya know what it means to have a light burning atop your home? It is safety, a place of refuge, seen by all as a signal that ye stand for something greater than this world, greater than us all.

"The beacon of hope it is, William love. Ours is a 'lighthouse' because your livin' made it so. You waited for me, love, as I do now for you. It's the Light of the World, he who lights inside of ya that brought me back to you."

Then I kissed my fair lady's hand, but she was gone. So I wrote down these words from a dream to give them to you, lad. It's the most important possession I have, the feelin' inside I mean. If I could, I'd cut it right out of my heart so you could have it, but it must be got through time, effort, and keeping the flame of truth alive.

The light that burns bright in the bosom of every good man and woman of hope is the true "Lighthouse Keeper." He is the Light of the World, just as my sweet Katie called him in the dream.

Long ago aboard a ship bound for America, I was asleep, sick, weary, and my Katie who went up on deck in grief of mind and body scribbled a note to me to come and "bring her a light."

I've done the best I could, not just for her but to every man. Now I say in partin', lad, be a good lightkeeper, take care of not only Anna and the wee one but the light inside yer bosom.

Don't let the evil, the shadows of darkness, take her away from you. Life's a test, lad. Run the race well.

A true lightkeeper shines his beam brightly on the one he loves forever, never lettin' go of his search for her love in return, and then, in the end, the love is better than it was in the beginnin'.

> *I love ya lad,*
> *Billie*

"Goodbye, sweet lightkeeper," Kathleen tearfully whispered as she kissed her father's forehead and stood to wheel him into the lighthouse and his final trip home.

As she carefully wheeled him around, the painting on her canvas caught her eye. The unfinished pier, the part she was trying to finish before she left for the docks an hour before, drew her to it.

It was the immense brightness, the glowing, dancing colors of amber; a luminescent gold, shimmering from the canvas that caught her eye.

In awe at the finished work, not completed by her own hand, her mouth fell open. There, surrounded by the fiery mix of light and pigment on the canvas, were two images she had not painted. They were standing on the pier, back to the shore, hand in hand.

And these two very distinct images were surrounded by the light, as if they had finally found a home.